Inspector Fehling was a very large policeman, but he prided himself on the precision and economy of his movements. A gorilla, but a very refined gorilla. His simplest action was an exhibition – a performance, and one had the uncomfortable feeling that applause was expected. He reminded Wycliffe of those extraordinary athletes who contort themselves improbably while balanced on a narrow beam. He emptied the contents of the girl's handbag on to the table. Compact, lipstick, comb, unmarked handkerchief, five pound notes and some loose change, a tube of aspirin, and a little pocket knife with a mother-of-pearl handle. 'There was a cigarette case and lighter in the pocket of her outside coat.'

Wycliffe pointed to the bundles of notes. 'How much?'

W.J. Burley lived near Newquay in Cornwall, and was a schoolmaster until he retired to concentrate on his writing. His many Wycliffe books include, most recently, *Wycliffe and the Guild of Nine*. He died in 2002.

By W.J. Burley

A Taste of Power
Three Toed Pussy
Death in Willow Pattern
Wycliffe and How to Kill a Cat
Wycliffe and the Guilt Edged Alibi
Death in a Salubrious Place
Death in Stanley Street
Wycliffe and the Pea Green Boat
Wycliffe and the Schoolgirls
The Schoolmaster
Wycliffe and the Scapegoat
The Sixth Day
Charles and Elizabeth
Wycliffe in Paul's Court
The House of Care
Wycliffe's Wild Goose Chase
Wycliffe and the Beales
Wycliffe and the Four Jacks
Wycliffe and the Quiet Virgin
Wycliffe and the Winsor Blue
Wycliffe and the Tangled Web
Wycliffe and the Cycle of Death
Wycliffe and the Dead Flautist
Wycliffe and the Last Rites
Wycliffe and the Dunes Mystery
Wycliffe and the Redhead
Wycliffe and the House of Fear
Wycliffe and the Guild of Nine

Wycliffe
AND
HOW TO KILL A CAT

W.J.Burley

An Orion paperback

First published in Great Britain in 1970
by Victor Gollancz Ltd
under the title *To Kill A Cat*
First published in paperback in 1993
by Arrow
This paperback edition published in 2006
by Orion Books Ltd
Orion House, 5 Upper St Martin's Lane,
London WC2H 9EA

An Hachette Livre UK company

A CIP catalogue record for this book is available
from the British Library.

ISBN 978-0-7528-8082-2

Printed and bound in Great Britain by
Clays Ltd, St Ives plc

The Orion Publishing Group's policy is to use papers that
are natural, renewable and recyclable products and
made from wood grown in sustainable forests. The logging
and manufacturing processes are expected to conform to
the environmental regulations of the country of origin.

www.orionbooks.co.uk

To Muriel—
collaborator, critic and wife

CHAPTER ONE

Detective Chief Superintendent Wycliffe, Area CID, in a fawn linen jacket, checked shirt and grey slacks, looked even less like a policeman than usual. He had the right, he was on holiday though paying a courtesy call at the local police station.

'Don't be all day, Charles!' Instructions from Helen, his wife.

'Back to lunch, dear. Promise!'

'Is Inspector Warren in?'

'No, sir, afraid not. Can I help?'

Wycliffe introduced himself. 'A friendly call, sergeant. The inspector and I used to be in the same squad and I thought I would look him up. I'm in the town on holiday.'

Ferocious grin, the best the station sergeant could manage in the way of charm. 'Inspector Warren has been ill with stomach ulcers for more than a month, sir.'

'I'm sorry to hear that.' Conversation languished.

'As you're from Headquarters, sir, you might like a word with . . .'

'No, this is unofficial, sergeant, I expect you've got enough to do at this time of year.'

'Run off our feet, sir.'

And that might have been that, had not a constable appeared from one of the offices, handed the sergeant a slip of paper and murmured something in his ear.

'Right! Get hold of the police surgeon and send him there. Tell Wilkins to stay with it and I'll contact Division.'

'Trouble, sergeant?' Wycliffe, on the point of leaving, lingered.

'Woman found dead in a hotel bedroom, sir. They called in one of our chaps from a patrol car and he's just radioed in.'

'Is that all?'

'Our man thinks there's a good reason to suspect foul play.'

'You mean that the woman has probably been murdered?'

'Yes, sir.'

'Then why not say so?'

The sergeant said nothing.

Wycliffe hesitated, then plunged. 'I'll take a look, where is it?'

'Marina Hotel, Dock Crescent, sir. It's a bit of a dump, they cater for merchant seamen mainly. We had trouble there once before.'

'What sort of trouble?'

'Seaman stabbed a tart, sir. A year or two back that was. I believe the place has changed hands since then.'

'Right! You get on to Division, tell them I'm on the spot and ask them not to roll out the waggon until they hear from me.'

'You'll want a car, sir.'

'I've got one.'

Outside the sun was shining. They were queueing for the beach buses, mothers with bulging picnic bags, kids trailing plastic spades, girls in brief summer dresses and some playsuits conscientiously displaying their navels. The superintendent in holiday attire was not out of place, but he attracted curious glances as he crossed the square to the car park. Perhaps it was because he looked pleased with life. Few people do, or are. In fact he was humming a little tune;

he caught himself doing it and wondered. The reason for his complacency would scarcely bear examination. True, it was warm and sunny; true, he was on holiday, but it was not these things, it was the prospect of a case which made him sing. He felt in his bones that he was at the beginning of a case which he would remember, one which would go into the books. To be brutally frank then, he was happy because a woman lay dead in a sleazy hotel bedroom. Did he delight in crime? Surely a vicarious pleasure in vice must be at least as reprehensible as indulgence?

He got into his nice new shining black Zodiac and eased his way into the line of traffic. He was secretly proud of his car though Helen said that it was a trifle vulgar. He liked to cruise slowly, almost silently, aware of the power he had boxed up, waiting only for the gentle pressure of his foot. In fact, he had the Rolls mentality without the Rolls pay packet.

Now he had to crawl through the impossibly narrow main street where a carelessly parked wheelbarrow can snarl everything up. Then the shops thinned and he was running along by the harbour with a row of large, terraced Victorian houses on his right. Just before he came to the docks some of the houses were calling themselves hotels and one of these was the Marina. A couple of tired looking Dracaenas in a weedy patch of gravel and a rusted slatted iron seat. The stucco was peeling off the pillars of the porch and a snake of Elastoplast sealed over a crack in the plate-glass of the swing doors. Constable Wilkins was waiting for him in the vestibule.

'The sergeant telephoned to expect you, sir.'

'Doctor arrived yet?'

'Not yet, sir.'

'Where is she?'

'Second floor, sir, a little passage off the landing leads

to the extension. It's the door on your left at the end of the passage.'

Wycliffe grunted. 'Wait there, send the doctor up when he comes. What about the inmates?'

'I've told them to stay in their rooms, sir. Most of them are out anyway.'

The staircase had some elegance of design but the carpet was so threadbare that pattern and texture had long since disappeared. Paper peeled off the walls and a faint sickly odour suggested dry rot. But the place seemed reasonably clean. He braced himself for what he might find. After twenty years in the force he was still not shockproof. He could have asked the constable but that was not his way, he liked to form his own impressions from the very start.

As he turned on the first landing to tackle the next flight, he made up his mind that the woman would be fortyish, fleshy, blonde and strangled. She would be lying in a tangle of bedding staring up at the ceiling, fish eyed, her face and neck heavily cyanosed. He had seen it all before. This place was a likely hunting ground for whores and if one of the sisterhood got herself murdered it was ten to one on strangulation, frenzied and brutal.

But he was wrong in most of his surmises.

The figure on the double bed was that of a girl, twenty-one or two at most. Slim, petite, she lay on her back, sprawled across the bed. She was naked but, though her posture was suggestive enough, there was something innocent and virginal about her. Her auburn hair was splayed on the pillow, golden in the sunshine, and it was easier to believe her asleep than dead – until he saw her face. Her face, turned towards the wall and hidden by her hair, had been battered. Without disturbing the body it was difficult to determine the extent and nature of her injuries but Wycliffe noticed at once that the amount of swelling and bruising was disproportionately small for the bone damage which had been done. The upper lip and an area round the left eye were encrusted with dried blood but there was no sign of a free flow. Wycliffe was no doctor but he had seen enough of violent death to know the probable answer to that one. The odds were that the facial injuries had been inflicted after death. In which case, how had she died? Perhaps the initial blow had killed her but it seemed unlikely. Would she have lain there waiting to be clubbed? Not unless she was asleep. But she was lying naked on top of the bed clothes . . .

Wycliffe bent closer to examine the neck and found what he half expected, a tale-telling bluish tinge below the surface of the skin and a faint bruising on either side of the trachea above the larynx. She had been strangled, but by someone who had restrained the impulse to unnecessary violence – or never known it. And that was odd in view of what must have followed. What sort of nut would strangle a girl with such finesse, then smash her face in?

But he was running ahead of himself, time enough to speculate when he had the views of the experts.

He looked round the room – a back room. The window, which had its top sash wedged open an inch or two, looked on to a small yard and a railway cutting beyond with the back gardens of a row of houses on the other side. An iron fire escape crossed diagonally just below the window. There were net blinds but the Regency striped curtains would not draw. The carpet was worn through in places and of no discernible pattern. A built-in clothes cupboard with a full length mirror in the door, a dressing table, an upholstered chair with loose stuffing – these, with the bed, made up the furniture. The girl's underclothes were strewn over the chair and a sleeveless frock in gay op-art material hung from a hanger hooked over the picture rail. A nightdress and a quilted dressing-gown lay in a heap on the floor by the bed. A white pig-skin travelling case, elegant and incongruous, stood by the dressing table which was littered with expensive looking cosmetics. Among the bottles and jars he noticed a few items of jewelry, a pair of earrings, a garnet bracelet and a silver clip with another red stone inset. He looked at everything but touched nothing.

He went out on to the landing when he heard footsteps on the stairs. The police surgeon, tall, slim, immaculate in pepper and salt suiting, iron-grey hair faultlessly parted, and bifocals. A questioning glance at Wycliffe's informal dress.

'Chief Superintendent Wycliffe? Dr Rashleigh. Where is she?'

'As little disturbance as possible if you please, doctor.'

A faint lift of the eyebrows. 'We must assume that we know our respective jobs, superintendent.'

'Perhaps. But don't move her!' Wycliffe snapped. Pompous ass! He went downstairs; doctors always put him in a bad temper. 'Constable!'

'Sir?'

'Radio information room for the murder squad, pathologist, forensic – the lot. Then find the proprietor.'

While he waited, Wycliffe opened a door labelled *Lounge*. A large front room with a bay window which could have been pleasant. Several upholstered armchairs in varying styles and stages of decay, an octagonal table in veneered wood of revolting aspect, a nickel-plated flower stand and plastic flowers. A black iron grate stuffed with crinkly red paper and an overmantle with fairground ornaments. The room reeked of stale tobacco. They would need somewhere to interview witnesses and this would have to be it. He decided to ask for some kitchen chairs to spite possible fleas.

The proprietor was a little man, bald on top with a fringe

of grey hair. He was thin except for his paunch, which he carried low. He was smoking a home-made cigarette and his lips were stained yellow. A near down-and-out like his premises, but he had lively brown eyes which missed nothing.

'What's your name?'

'Ernest Piper.'

Wycliffe lowered himself on to the arm of one of the chairs. 'Who is she, Mr Piper?'

The little man raised a hand to his ear and stroked the lobe. 'According to the register she's Mrs Slatterly. Address given, W1.'

'When did she arrive?'

'Sunday evening, she's been here three nights.'

'Alone?'

He nodded. 'She said she was waiting for her husband to join her.'

'And did he?'

'Not to my knowledge, he didn't.'

'Had she booked in advance?'

'Telephone call the day before to reserve a double for three or four nights.'

'Not a common experience for you.'

Piper put in some more time fiddling with his ear. 'I don't know what you mean.'

The superintendent took out his pipe and began to fill it. He was entering into the spirit of the thing, beginning to get its flavour. 'I mean that you don't get many bookings, certainly not from husbands and their wives.'

A slow grin revealing blackened teeth. 'I don't have to draw pictures for you, do I?'

'What was your impression of her when she arrived?'

'Classy. Pretty too, a real eye catcher. Pity she got spoilt like that. To be frank, I couldn't make out what she was doing in a place like this . . .' He hesitated then added in a burst of confidence, 'Look, superintendent, I got nothing to hide in this business and I hope you'll bear in mind that I'm being frank.'

Wycliffe struck a match and lit his pipe, puffing great clouds of smoke towards the ceiling. 'We'll see. Did she have any visitors?'

'Not to my knowledge.'

'Which doesn't take us very far.'

Piper shrugged. 'Well, you know how it is.'

'Did she go out much?'

'I passed her in the hall a few times. In any case she had to go out for food, we don't do meals other than breakfast.'

'Any mail?'

'One letter waiting for her when she arrived.'

'Postmark?'

'I didn't notice.'

'Who found her this morning?'

'Kathy, the girl who does the rooms.'

'When?'

Piper looked at his watch, a silver turnip which he took from a pocket in his unbuttoned waistcoat. 'About an hour ago. Say half nine. Kathy came to me in the kitchen and said, "I think something's happened to the girl in fifteen. I think she's dead." '

'Just like that.'

Piper nodded. 'Just like that, Kathy don't scare all that easy.'

'Then?'

'I went up to take a look.' He relit his cigarette which had gone out.

'Touch anything?'

He shook his head. 'Only her – just to see if she had really croaked. I didn't see her face at first. Of course she'd been dead several hours, I should think.'

'You know about such things?'

'I seen a bit.'

'How long since you were last inside?'

A moment of reflection. 'Must be all of ten years.'

'Immoral earnings?'

He nodded. 'No violence though. I never been done for violence.'

Wycliffe noted and approved the precision of statement. The two men smoked placidly in complete accord.

'She was no trollop, super.'

Wycliffe sighed. 'They all have to start.'

The doctor interrupted them, shirt-sleeved and peevish, 'I suppose there is somewhere I can wash in this place?'

'Down the passage on the right, doctor, I'll show you.' Courtesy and service à la Marina! Wycliffe chuckled. He felt better and better. It wasn't crime which gave him pleasure, it was people. He made himself comfortable in the armchair. To hell with fleas!

Dr Rashleigh came back alone. 'I suppose you have notified the pathologist?'

'Of course! Perhaps you will be good enough to look in again when he is here?'

'Very well!' Rashleigh was still stuffy. 'But you may wish to hear my preliminary conclusions?'

Pretentious bastard! 'Certainly, doctor.'

Rashleigh smoothed his tie (Greyhounds 1934). 'I don't want to be too specific, but I think I may say that death was probably due to strangulation. The indications of asphyxia are slight and though there are marks on the neck they are faint.' He squinted up at the ceiling through his bifocals as though reading his lines there and mumbled something about 'vagal inhibition'. Then he went on, 'The facial injuries were almost certainly inflicted after death. As to time of death, I would say that she has been dead from eight to twelve hours.'

'Between ten and two, then?'

'That would certainly agree with my preliminary findings, superintendent. If I were pressed I should incline towards the earlier time.'

'Very helpful, doctor. Anything else?'

Rashleigh hesitated. 'The girl was not a virgin, superintendent.'

Big deal! Surely he must know if anybody did that virginity beyond the age of twenty is a wasting asset?

'In fact, certain signs lead me to suppose that sexual intercourse probably took place shortly before death.'

'Not after?'

Rashleigh looked flustered. 'I'm not in a position to answer that question on the evidence I have seen.'

Surely the old goat must realize that it mattered! Never mind, the pathologist would see to all that.

When the divisional inspector arrived with his squad he found Wycliffe alone. He was standing beside the window, staring out at the docks. Born and reared and having lived most of his life in the Midlands, the sea and all that pertained to it fascinated him. Those tankers with their ugly grey hulls had probably rounded the Cape not so long ago on their way from some sun-scorched oil port in the Gulf . . .

Inspector Fehling coughed. He had not previously met the chief superintendent, who was a comparative newcomer to the area. His first impression was unfavourable and the inspector set great store by his first impressions. Wycliffe did not even look like a policeman, it was difficult to believe that he was tall enough and he seemed almost frail. A teacher, some kind of academic, perhaps a parson, but never a policeman.

'Inspector Fehling, sir.'

'How do you spell it?'

'F – E – H . . .'

'Ah, the solution, not a lack of success.'

'Sir?'

'Fehling's solution – Prussian blue stuff they used to use to test urine. Never mind, an unusual name, Inspector.'

'So they tell me. Now, do I have your permission to go ahead, sir?'

Wycliffe smiled as though at a secret joke. 'By all means. The pathologist should be here at any minute and the forensic people will be on their way. Let me know if you find anything – I shall be here.' When Fehling reached the door he called him back. 'Mr Fehling, I object to working in the middle of a circus – no cars outside this building. They must park on the car park down the street; and no uniformed men in evidence . . .'

Fehling was shocked. 'But there are several of our vehicles out there now . . .'

'Then please get them moved – damn quick!'

When Fehling was gone Wycliffe returned to the window. Delegation is a magic word. When you have the rank you can get out of almost any job you don't like doing. Not that chief superintendents are expected to search rooms, look for prints or photograph corpses. He had done his share in the past but never with much enthusiasm or faith. You may need such evidence to convict a man but crimes are about people and relationships. Wycliffe was of a contemplative disposition and he liked, on occasion, to talk. He was remarkable in that he had contrived to turn these dubious attributes into professional assets.

'He said you might like a cup of coffee.' A sleek, black-haired little West Indian girl carrying a tray with a cup of coffee on it, milk and sugar. She looked no more than sixteen but was probably twenty.

'Thanks, I would. Who are you?'

'I'm Kathy – Kathy Johnson – I work here.'

'It was you who found the dead girl?'

She nodded. Another surprise, he had expected some superannuated old pro with swollen legs and carpet slippers. 'I found her.'

'You sleep on the premises?'

'In one of the attics, yes.' She spoke with the attractive staccato precision of her people and she had a gravity of expression and demeanour which gave special weight to all she said.

'What do you know of the dead girl?'

'Not much. She was very pretty. I see her on the stairs once or twice and wish her good morning or good afternoon but that is all except one time . . .'

'What happened?'

She put her hand to her forehead in a quick gesture of recollection. 'I think it was on the first evening she is here, a man come and ask for her. No! it was the next evening – Monday.'

'Did this man ask for her by name?'

'Pardon?'

'Did this man say, "I want to speak to Mrs Slatterly" – that is the name she gave in the register isn't it?'

'Mrs Slatterly, that is right. No, I find him in the hall looking at the register and when I ask him what it is that he wants, at first he is unwilling to say then he say, "This Mrs Slatterly, is she young with auburn hair?" and I say, "Yes, but she is out".'

'What then?'

'He thinks for some time then he ask if there is a telephone in her room.' Kathy laughed at the very idea. 'When I say that there is not, he go off without another word.'

'Have you seen him since?'

'No, I do not see him again.'

'When you told Mrs Slatterly of his visit, did she seem worried?'

The little brown nose wrinkled. 'No, not worried.'

'Why don't you sit down?'

'Thank you.' She perched herself on the edge of one of the chairs, her tray in her lap. 'I do not think her name was Mrs Slatterly.'

'Why not?'

'When I have to tell her about the man who come to see her she is half way up the stairs, you understand?'

Wycliffe nodded.

'I say, "Mrs Slatterly!" and although she is sure to hear me she does not turn round. Twice I say it, then I have to go up after her.'

'You are a clever girl.'

'Thank you.'

'About this man, what was he like?'

'Not very tall, a bit fat, and he wore a dark suit with little stripes. It fitted very good, very smart and expensive looking. His hair is sandy coloured.'

'Oldish?'

'Pardon?'

'How old do you think he was?'

'Forty, maybe a little more. He is red in the face a little, perhaps he has had too much to drink, you understand?'

'Perfectly; anything else?'

She frowned. 'There was something about his face, something a little strange, like it was fixed.'

'You mean that his face lacked expression?'

She hesitated then gave up. 'I cannot say what it is that I mean, I am sorry.'

'But you would know him again if you saw him?'

'Of course!'

'Thank you, you are an excellent witness but you may have to say all this again so that it can be written down.'

'That is all right.' She got up, picked up his cup and was at the door when he said, 'You never saw her talking to anyone, I suppose?'

She turned, frowning. 'I almost forget. Yesterday morning when I am making the bed in one of the front rooms I happen to look out of the window. Mrs Slatterly was standing on the pavement by the gate talking to a man.'

'The same one?'

'No, I told you I do not see him again. This is a very tall thin man and, I think, younger, but I could not see him well. I know that he had on a cap and a mackintosh, but I cannot tell you any more.'

'Did they stay talking for long?'

She shook her head. 'I cannot say, I did not stop to watch.'

Progress, or so it seemed. It might not be too difficult to run down the chap in the natty pinstripe – if he was a local. Perhaps Fehling would find firm evidence of the girl's identity by the time he was through upstairs. It was more than likely. But if not . . . Wycliffe sighed and returned to the window, refilled his pipe and lit it. Never go to meet trouble. Two of the dockside cranes were performing complex evolutions, moving along their tracks and swinging their jibs in perfect harmony. Why did they do it? They never seemed to lift anything. Choreography by the shop steward.

Back to the sandy-haired chap in the pinstripes. If he had intended to kill the girl he wouldn't have made himself so conspicuous unless he was a kink. If he killed her it was probably unpremeditated, a sudden flare of anger or lust. Most murders by strangulation were like that but, a big but, the murderer invariably uses force far in excess of what is needed to kill. In this case there was remarkable restraint and restraint implies forethought. But what about the maniacal attack on the girl's face after death? It didn't add up. Wycliffe remembered a young thug in his old manor who made a study of the technique of strangulation, treating it as an art form. Four girls died before he was caught red-handed with the fifth, and none of them had showed any outward sign of the cause of death. Broadmoor. Detained at Her Majesty's Pleasure. He remembered the case with acute loathing, he had hated that youth and he hoped that Her Majesty would get a hell of a lot of pleasure. Violence of any sort appalled him and senseless self-indulgent violence left him biting his nails.

The pathologist and the forensic people arrived. Wycliffe had met the same team before and they exchanged amiable greetings, then the newcomers went about their business with that air of bored indifference which is their professional equivalent to the bedside manner. The little room was overcrowded and stuffy, but each man knew his job and scarcely a word was spoken. Wycliffe waited on the landing with the police photographers who had already taken pictures of the undisturbed room and were waiting to take more when the pathologist gave the word for the removal of the body.

It took them less than an hour. Dr Franks, the pathologist, a chubby little man, always in a hurry, bustled out. 'Ready now, superintendent. Perhaps you will get one of your chaps to bring up the shell.'

The girl's body would be put into a plastic shell, a temporary coffin, to be carted off to the mortuary.

Franks went into the bathroom and began to run lots of water. Wycliffe could hear him whistling to himself as he washed. It was all in the day's work for him too. 'Bit of a bug-house this, isn't it? What's a kid like that doing in this sort of dump? – Don't tell me, I'd rather keep my illusions. Where the hell is the soap? She was strangled all right. Bit of a fancy job or else a lucky hold by a tyro. Perhaps it was unlucky. Pressure on the jugulars. Even that mightn't have killed her by itself. I'll tell you more this afternoon, but not much. This bloody towel . . . For Christ's sake send somebody for a clean towel . . . Intercourse, as they say, had taken place – *was* taking place for all I know. Not the usual thing though, is it? Then he bashes her face in afterwards. Dear me! A nasty fellow he must be!'

A constable arrived with a fresh towel.

'Ah, that's better! I suppose Rashleigh told you how long she's been dead?'

'Between ten last night and two this morning.'

Franks nodded. 'I'd say after midnight.' He ran a pocket comb through his thinning hair. 'Are you going to join us this afternoon?'

'I shall be looking in.'

Wycliffe went downstairs to the lounge so as not to be in the way. A few minutes later he heard the men carrying her body down. The siren at the docks wailed. Half past twelve; lunchtime. A minute later a flood of bicycles burst through the gates and jammed the road outside. Fortunately they seemed too anxious to get home to bother about what was going on in the Marina.

Fehling came in looking important, a large briefcase under his arm. He whisked the flower stand with its plastic flowers on to the floor, removed the table runner and dusted the table top with a yellow duster from his briefcase. Then he displayed his finds. A photograph in a transparent polythene envelope with blue circles to indicate finger-prints, ten bundles of used pound notes, and a handbag.

'I'm not quite through yet, sir, but I doubt if there's much more of importance. Forensic have been over this lot.'

Inspector Fehling was a very large policeman, but he prided himself on the precision and economy of his movements. A gorilla, but a very refined gorilla. His simplest action was an exhibition – a performance, and one had the uncomfortable feeling that applause was expected. He reminded Wycliffe of those extraordinary athletes who contort themselves improbably while balanced on a narrow beam. He emptied the contents of the girl's handbag on to the table. Compact, lipstick, comb, unmarked handkerchief, five pound notes and some loose change, a tube of aspirin, and a little pocket knife with a mother-of-pearl handle. 'There was a cigarette case and lighter in the pocket of her outside coat.'

Wycliffe pointed to the bundles of notes. 'How much?'

'A thousand pounds, sir. It was in a drawer of the chest under some of her clothing.'

'Anything else?'

Fehling considered. 'Her clothes, of course, they seem to be of pretty good quality, a few pieces of jewelry and a sachet of oral contraceptives. She wore a ring but there is only a superficial mark on her finger so she probably put it on for the occasion.' He produced the ring in a plastic envelope; a gold wedding ring in an antique style, engraved inside with a monogram: *W & J*, entwined. A moment of hesitation, then, 'That room had been searched before we got there, sir, I'd take my oath on it.'

'They couldn't have been looking for money.'

Fehling was ponderously judicial. 'That's what puzzles

me. You wouldn't think they would pass up a thousand quid in singles.'

'Is it possible that they wanted to remove anything that might identify her?'

'Could be! Could be, indeed, sir.' Fehling nodded his great head in approval. 'The West Indian girl says there was a framed photograph of the dead woman on the dressing table, but it's not there now.'

Wycliffe picked up the photograph in the plastic envelope. A half-length portrait of a young man with an electric guitar slung over his shoulder. A thin-faced youth with vacant eyes and the gloomy constipated look common to his kind. No signature, nothing written on the back. It was a studio portrait or the work of a good amateur but too glossy, like the publicity handouts from the big stars.

'Are you an authority on the Charts, Mr Fehling?'

'The charts, sir?'

'The Top Twenty.'

Fehling was disdainful. 'I'm afraid I'm too busy to bother with that nonsense.'

Wycliffe pushed the photograph towards him. 'Then you'd better consult an expert. If he's one of the idols he probably has nothing to do with our case, but if he's the boyfriend then we badly need his help.'

'What sort of expert would you suggest, sir?'

Wycliffe counted ten to himself then answered mildly, 'Try Kathy Johnson.'

'Kathy?'

'Kathy Johnson, the girl who seems to do all the work round here.'

'Oh, the West Indian girl!'

Wycliffe sighed. 'One more thing, the proprietor has got form but I don't want it rammed down his neck. Keep him sweet, he could be very useful.' Wycliffe began to fill his pipe. 'What do you make of it so far?'

The inspector picked up a bundle of notes and flicked them through as though he was about to perform a conjuring trick. 'This money suggests only one thing to me, sir – dope.'

'You think she was here to buy?'

Fehling hunched his immense shoulders. 'Stands to reason! I mean, this is a seaport, she's staying in a sleazy boarding house run for merchant seamen and she's got a thousand in used notes. She wouldn't be selling, would she? Not in this neck of the woods. I reckon we're on to something, sir.'

'In that case, the deal didn't go through – she was still in possession of the money. So she wasn't killed for it. So what was she killed for?'

This extraordinary verbal gymnastic did not baffle the inspector. 'Her boy friend probably knows something about that!'

'This laddie in the picture?' He shook his head. 'In that case we are dealing with two separate crimes both centred on the girl. It's not impossible but William wouldn't like it – neither do I.'

'William, sir?'

'Of Occam, a thirteenth-century gent who enunciated the axiom that in logic, entities must not be multiplied.'

'Ah!'

'Useful to remind oneself that the simplest possible explanation is probably the right one.'

'Quite so, sir.' (Christ! Where do they dig 'em up?) 'Well, sir, what next?'

Wycliffe opened the door and called, 'Kathy!' When she came he showed her the photograph of the boy with the guitar. 'Know him, Kathy?'

'I do not know that boy, superintendent.'

'Would you if he was famous?'

She grinned. 'Oh, yes! I have all their photographs in my room.' Wycliffe thanked her. 'And Kathy! I want you to write out a description of the man you found going through the register. Take your time over it and make it as complete as you can, then give it to Mr Fehling.'

Kathy went and he turned to Fehling. 'Have you found the blunt instrument?'

'Sir?'

'Whatever was used to hit her.'

'Ah. No, sir, we haven't found it, but there's a door stop missing. The door doesn't fasten properly from the inside and Piper put a seven pound brass weight there to keep it shut. Apparently it's one of those with a ring in the top to hold it by.'

'So, whoever it was didn't come prepared.'

Fehling chuckled. 'And it's not every bedroom in which you can count on finding a brass weight handy . . .'

Wycliffe looked at him blankly. 'You'd better set about finding that weight, hadn't you, Mr Fehling? And Mr Fehling, pass the word round, I don't want it known that the girl was disfigured. We'll keep that to ourselves for the moment.' He got up, searching in his pockets for sixpences for the telephone. Fehling stopped him at the door. 'There's one more thing, I forgot it – this, I found it under her bed.'

'What is it?'

He held out a shining ball the size of a marble. 'It's a steel ball-bearing, probably nothing to do with the girl. I expect it fell out of the pocket of the chap who had the room before her.'

Wycliffe took the little ball and slipped it into his pocket. 'I expect you're right.'

CHAPTER TWO

Wycliffe's hotel also overlooked the harbour, but higher up the estuary, away from the docks, next to the yacht club. The dining room was built out over the water and the racing dinghies often sailed brazenly close to the windows before going about. Wycliffe poured himself another glass of Chablis. 'Very pleasant wine, this, in fact they do us very well here altogether, very well.'

Helen laughed. 'Too well for your waist line, I think.'

He was feeling mellow after a good lunch. The water was like a mirror and if you looked with half closed eyes the whole scene dissolved into a living mosaic of colour, blue, yellow, red and white hulls with the green hill-side beyond. It would be pleasant to hire a boat and potter about the harbour for the afternoon. There was a little village of grey stone houses across the water and it would be fun to tie up at the jetty and stroll round the village, perhaps to have tea there. But he had a photo-graph in his pocket, a photograph of a young man who might, just possibly, be a murderer. He had put off telling Helen, not that she would fuss, she had been too long a policeman's wife, but it might have taken the edge off the enjoyment of their lunch.

'Something cropped up this morning.'

'I thought as much.'

'How could you?'

'You had that half smug, half guilty look I know so well, and you were late for lunch. Is it serious?'

'Murder. I should have been sent for anyway.'

Helen sighed. 'Oh, well, perhaps they will let you charge your hotel bill.'

Comforting woman.

As a concession to convention he changed his linen jacket and slacks for a lightweight suit of worsted and at two o'clock he was walking along the narrow twisting main street, smoking his pipe, one of the crowd returning to work. He would have liked to have been really a part of it, to have exchanged familiar greetings with the people he passed, to have known why the shutters were up at number forty-four, why the tobacconist at thirty-six was wearing a black arm band and the real story behind the newspaper placard which read: COUNCILLOR HILL WITHDRAWS.

This was a credible size for a community, you could identify yourself with it, live its life.

In the newspaper office a mini-skirted girl took time off to be polite. 'This is only a branch office but if you'd like to wait you could see Mr Brown, the local reporter. He's out to his lunch.'

In course of time Mr Brown arrived smelling of his liquid lunch, a red-headed young man, breezily efficient. 'Always ready to help the police, superintendent, what can we do for you?'

In a little office which had a desk, a chair, a typewriter, a telephone and nothing else, Wycliffe produced his photograph.

Brown studied it critically. 'Nasty business at the Marina, superintendent.'

'Very.'

'Is this the bloke?'

'Not as far as I know. Have you seen him before?'

As Brown spoke a cigarette danced up and down between his lips. 'They're all alike, aren't they? All the same

I should probably know him if he was a local lad. Can we print this? Say it was found on the scene of the crime?'

Wycliffe retrieved the photograph. 'We shall put it on the regional telly tonight. If that doesn't work I shall probably circulate it, you can print it then.'

'Who was she, super?'

Wycliffe shrugged. 'I wish I knew. Perhaps you could help, keep your eyes and ears open.'

Brown nodded. 'On a quid pro quo basis. I got precious little out of your chap at the Marina.'

'I'll see to it personally.'

'Thanks.'

'Any time!' The superintendent strolled out into the sunshine and this time he made for the car park.

He drove in a leisurely fashion the ten miles to the county town, infuriating other drivers who could only pass at those rare spots where the road had been straightened and widened. It took him twenty-three minutes. The white Jag chuntering behind would probably have done it in thirteen. Ten minutes lost! Save fivepence on the large packet! The kind of economics Wycliffe would never understand.

The afternoon sun beat down on the hospital campus so that the asphalt was soft underfoot and he was grateful for the cool tiled corridors of the pathology building. He made for the mortuary. It was overrun with people, some of whom had been at the Marina earlier. The police photographers were there with the tools of their trade, the people from forensic and a covey of policemen in and out of uniform. Wycliffe had arranged to meet some of his own Area squad there and he saw Chief Inspector James Gill pushing his way through the crowd towards him.

'Long time no see, sir! Must be all of a week!' Gill was young for his rank, craggy, tough and cynical enough to make Wycliffe feel, by contrast, comfortably warm-hearted. He liked working with Gill and had sent for him on this occasion.

'Who's with you?'

'Hartley, Wills and Manders, all we could spare. What's the Divisional set-up?'

Wycliffe shrugged. 'You'll meet Inspector Fehling directly. Impressive – that's the word, Jimmy, impressive.'

They were making their way through gossiping groups to the far end of the room where Franks and two of his assistants were working on the body of the dead girl. The acrid fishy smell of formalin was strong.

'Anything for me?'

Franks looked up. 'As far as the girl is concerned, nothing you'll want to hear. She was healthy, well nourished, between twenty and twenty-two, she had never given birth. No scars, no nice identifiable old fractures. She has a large mole on her left breast, her teeth have been well cared for, no extractions and only two fillings . . .'

Dr Bell of forensic joined them by the table. 'And there's no joy from the clothing either – there isn't much of it anyway.' He was bald headed, a little wisp of a man, with an oversized pipe which he sucked whether it was lit or not – 'Nipple fixation', he called it. 'Our job would be a pushover if women still wore calico drawers and shifts.'

'I can tell you one thing,' Franks said. He always saved the best till last. 'The man who made love to her is AB.' He looked absurdly pleased with himself, like a little boy who has just said his party piece. 'I ran the usual grouping tests on the seminal fluid and for once we hit the jack-pot.'

Wycliffe was unimpressed, or pretended to be. 'Big deal! If I remember rightly, about three per cent of the population are in the AB group, so, leaving women and children aside, that gives us a round half million suspects in the UK to choose from.'

Franks's baby face wrinkled into a grin. 'You chaps want your job done for you! As it is we do most of it.'

Wycliffe looked down at the figure on the dissecting table. He was hardened by long usage, but it was in any case difficult to connect this gruesome cadaver with the eye-catching girl who had booked in at the Marina on Sunday night. It was that girl he wanted to know about, her living and her loving and the web of circumstance which had finally put an end to them both. He had to put the clock back to Sunday night at least, probably much further, and try to live with her that borrowed time.

He sent Chief Inspector Gill in search of the police photographer. 'I want you to work on your shots of the face and with Dr Franks's help, bring her alive. Let's have a photograph we can publish, one that her friends will recognize.'

Both men were doubtful but they agreed to try; and Kathy, Wycliffe said, would check the result.

Chief Inspector Gill rode back with Wycliffe in his nice new Zodiac to be put in the picture. Gill watched the countryside gliding sedately by and listened. It was one of Wycliffe's consolations that he didn't have to spell everything out for Gill; they had evolved a kind of conversational shorthand which, despite differences of temperament, they could use because their logical processes were similar.

'Three sets of prints on the photograph of the guitarist, one set belonging to the girl. Copies have gone to Area and to CRO.'

'So if he's got form, there's a chance, otherwise . . .'

'It's possible that none of the dabs are the killer's anyway.'

Gill let another mile or so slide by – they were trailing a

green double-decker bus at twenty with a queue of traffic behind waiting in vain for Wycliffe to make a move.

'Been this way before, Jim?'

'No sir, first visit. Seems pleasant enough, trees and all that.'

'You should bring your wife and kids down for a holiday.'

'Holiday? What's that? I thought it was something they gave to school kids. Going back to the case, this grouping test of Franks's, is it the same as a blood test?'

'Same thing.'

'Then it could help?'

Wycliffe drew to a halt behind the bus which had stopped to set down passengers. 'If we had a line-up of suspects it might, but we don't even know who the girl is. That's our first job and our best bet there is . . .'

'The laddie with the guitar.'

'Exactly. With any luck the photograph should be in all the papers tomorrow and it might be on television tonight.'

The cars behind had taken advantage of the bus stop and were streaming past. Finally the bus got going again and Wycliffe fell in behind.

'I suppose you couldn't pass that thing, sir? The diesel fumes . . .'

Wycliffe seemed surprised. 'Do they bother you? Anyway it's hardly worth it now, we're just coming into the town.'

They were cruising along a suburban road lined with Dracaenas and villas in a bewildering variety of architectural styles, each with its Bed and Breakfast sign. A canvas banner between two lamp-posts advertised a summer show at the Council's theatre.

Inspector Fehling had been busy establishing a murder

hunt HQ at the station. The recreation room had been cleared and equipped with tables and chairs, an epidiascope and a slide projector. A projection screen was fixed to one of the walls flanked by maps of the town and surrounding areas. Telephone engineers were busy installing additional instruments. Fehling looked at his achievement with pride.

'What are the magic lanterns for?' Wycliffe asked.

'A slide projector and epidiascope, sir, for projecting transparencies and prints.'

'Ah!'

'Visual aids, I think they call them, sir,' Gill said. 'All the rage in progressive forces.'

Opening off the main room were two little rooms which Fehling had set aside for the 'brass'. 'You take your choice, sir,' he offered generously, 'but this one is a bit bigger so I've taken the liberty of putting the reports there.' He pointed to a wire tray on the table containing an alarming bundle of typescript.

Wycliffe sat himself in one of the bentwood chairs on the wrong side of the desk and Gill chose the other. Fehling was left standing.

'For God's sake, sit down, Mr Fehling!'

So the inspector had to fit himself into the armchair behind the desk and he bulged over the arms. He started to sort the reports. Obviously he was good at paper work, which is the way to get on. If you make enough copies of bugger-all people think it and you must be important. Wycliffe filled his pipe, refused any papers and said, 'Tell us about it, Mr Fehling.'

Fehling passed a great hand over his brow and back over his thinning curls. 'There is only one new lead so far. You remember the house on the other side of the railway cutting?'

Wycliffe nodded. 'Their backs overlook the back of the hotel.'

'Exactly, they're good class houses, sir – respectable.'

'What's that got to do with it? Are you thinking of buying one?'

'Just that they're the sort of people who make reliable witnesses.'

Wycliffe questioned the assumption but said nothing. In his experience the more respectable people were, the more they had to hide. They didn't want to be mixed up in anything that wasn't quite nice.

'The lady at number twenty-six, a Mrs Foster, says that at a little after midnight she happened to be looking out of her landing window when she saw someone standing on the fire escape of the hotel.'

'Man or woman?'

'She thinks it was a man though she could only see a silhouette against the lighted window.'

'Which window?'

'Top floor of the extension, she says. It must have been the girl's room or the bathroom.'

'What was he doing?'

'Just standing there according to her. She says she watched him for nearly ten minutes.'

'The window of the girl's room won't open.'

'No, sir, it's screwed up.'

'And the curtains won't draw.' Wycliffe lit his pipe and blew clouds of smoke ceilingwards. 'What was she doing looking out of her window at that time of night?'

'I don't know, sir, but she says she's complained on several occasions to the police about goings on in that place.'

'I'll bet!' He caught Gill looking at him quizzically, wondering why he was knocking poor old Fehling who seemed to be doing a pretty good job. He hardly knew himself, not until he stopped to think, then he knew. It was the tacit assumption of Fehling and his like that the world is divided into two camps, the good and the bad, the respectable and the contemptible, the cops and the robbers. Never would Fehling look at one of his victims and say, 'There but for the grace of God . . .'

'Anything else?'

Fehling looked aggrieved, as well he might. 'The other two rooms on that floor of the extension, sir – one was occupied by an elderly tradesman sent down from Newcastle by his firm to do some special job on that cruise liner which is being refitted in the yard.'

'Could he tell you anything?'

'Nothing. He said he'd had a few drinks and slept like a log. The other room – the room next to the girl's – was let to a young man waiting to join his ship when she docks on Sunday. He was the worse for drink too and his recollections are hazy. But he had a girl with him . . .'

'What does she say?'

Fehling stroked his smooth chin which, in a few years, would extend in rolls down his neck. 'We haven't found her yet, sir. He picked her up in one of the pubs and he can't remember much about her except that she cleared off early this morning.'

'What about Piper?'

'Sir?'

'The proprietor of the place – what does he say about the girl?'

'Says he had no idea she was there, if he had he would have thrown her out. Respectable house, all that malarkey.'

'So what are you doing about it?'

'My chaps will be doing the rounds of the pubs tonight.'

'No.'

'Sir?'

'I said no, I expect they've got something better to do than a subsidized pub crawl.'

Fehling raised his eyes to the ceiling and pursed his lips. Chief Inspector Gill was enjoying himself.

'What about the other people staying in the place – anybody suspicious?'

Fehling fished some papers out of the wire tray. 'Here are the reports, sir.'

'Tell me about them, Mr Fehling.'

'Well, sir, there were nine other people staying in the hotel. All were men and all have been questioned by my chaps. They've given credible accounts of themselves, but we're checking, and they've been told not to leave the town without notifying us. Most of them – all but two, in fact – are waiting to join their ships. They've got seamen's books which seem to be in order.'

'What about the other two?'

'Lorry driver and his mate, sir, down here to pick up some turbine rotors which have to go back to the works for balancing.'

Wycliffe stood up. 'Well, I'm off! I'll leave you and Chief Inspector Gill together. No doubt you'll find that you have much in common.'

'Christ! Is he always like that?'

Gill looked at the door which had barely closed behind the Chief Superintendent. 'Mostly, but you'll get used to it.'

'I don't know that I want to,' Fehling grumbled. 'It's like tight boots, there don't seem to be much point in starting.'

Wycliffe left his car on the park and walked in the direction of the main street. It was just on six according to the clock over the post office, and visitors were streaming off the quay, returning from the afternoon boat trips, making for their lodgings and dinner. The children trailed behind and were scolded while the toddlers had to be carried on daddys' shoulders. Wycliffe watched it all with interest and approval. He never tired of watching people, people about their business and their pleasure. Some men watched animals, building little hides to spy on badgers, birds or deer, but Wycliffe could not understand them. From a window on to a street, from a seat in a pub or a park, or strolling round a fairground, it was possible to observe a far more varied species, more complex, more intelligent, more perceptive and vastly richer in the pattern of their emotional response.

The narrow main street was almost deserted, the shops closed, the pubs and fried fish bars just opening their doors but with no customers as yet. Wycliffe ambled along window shopping. The bookshop he had noticed before, an especially good bookshop for a small town. Two large windows, one devoted to new and the other to secondhand books, well displayed and priced. A card invited inspection of *twenty thousand secondhand books inside – many of antiquarian interest and importance*. He promised himself that he would find time to spend an hour there. Good bookshops were getting all too rare. He noticed the name on the signboard:

W.P. COLLINS & SON.
NEW AND SECOND HAND BOOKSELLERS
Estab: 1847

Good for the Collinses!

He made his way through the street on towards the docks and the Marina. Apart from a few people on the pavement gawping, it looked serenely undisturbed. He pushed his way through the swing glass doors and found a constable in the hall. 'Is the room sealed?'

'Yes, sir.'

'Then report back, no need to waste your time here.' The constable went. 'Anybody home?' Silence. An appetizing smell led him by the nose to the kitchen. In better days it had been a conservatory and some of the smaller panes were red or blue or orange glass so that gay splashes of colour cropped up in unexpected places. Piper was seated at a large table covered with oilcloth, reading a racing paper and eating curried stew with a spoon. Opposite him, sitting bolt upright, prim as a maiden aunt at the Vicar's teaparty, Kathy, eating her stew very skilfully, with a fork.

Ernie Piper was too old a hand to be put off his food by a policeman. He looked up and grinned. 'Sit yourself down, superintendent, what can we do for you?'

'You like curry, superintendent? I make it myself and there is plenty.'

Wycliffe realized that he was hungry. 'It smells good!'

'She cooks like an angel,' Piper said. 'That's why I keep you, isn't it, Kathy?'

Kathy smiled but said nothing.

The curry was good – and hot. He had to suck in his breath after the first mouthful. Piper laughed. 'Try some bread, superintendent,' and he passed the board with the best part of a two pound loaf on it. 'She makes her own bread too. It makes going straight worth while.'

For a time they ate in silence. Piper opened a couple of bottles of beer and decanted them into glasses. Wycliffe wondered what Inspector Fehling would make of it if he could see them now.

'Who was the girl in sixteen last night?'

Piper shrugged, 'I told the inspector . . .'

'I know what you told the inspector, I also know your sort, my lad. Is your front door locked at night?'

'Well, no . . .'

'And is there, or is there not, a board in the hall which shows the rooms which are occupied?'

'I told you, I'm going straight, superintendent.' Piper took a great gulp of beer and wiped his lips with the back of his hand.

Wycliffe grinned. 'That's as may be but you're not going soft! Are you trying to tell me that any pick-up can have a free night's lodging and enjoy the other amenities of your establishment if she cares to bring her bloke here?'

Piper looked sheepish. 'Well no, but I can't stop the chaps who lodge here bringing back a bird if they feel that way, can I? I mean this isn't a Sunday school.'

Wycliffe had finished his curry and he was fiddling with the crusty top of the loaf. He broke off a generous chunk and began to nibble. It reminded him of when he used to be sent to buy bread when he was a kid – before they turned it into sponge rubber.

'Have some butter with it?'

'Not likely!' He chewed happily. 'I wouldn't like to be the girl who came back here with one of your boarders if she wasn't on your visiting list or if she didn't leave the proper cut. Where do they put it? Do they drop it in the potted palm as they go out?'

Piper chuckled. 'I'll say one thing for you, you know the score! It was Millie Ford, 46, Castle Hill. She's a good girl so don't you go upsetting her.'

'And don't you push your luck!' Wycliffe growled.

It was a mellow evening, a golden light over the harbour, softening the colours, blurring the outlines, the water still and gleaming.

Castle Hill was on his way back to the hotel, a minor hump in the low lying ground which fringes the harbour. You climb steeply from the main street between two rows of small and, for the most part, derelict shops, then the road falls away more slowly to the level of the harbour and the hotel. Millie lived over a shop which displayed a dusty collection of china and glass ornaments calling them, hopefully, antiques. The shop was shut so he knocked at the side door. An immensely fat woman across the street, standing in her doorway, shouted, 'You got to go up, dearie!' Despite all his years in the Force he was embarrassed.

The door opened on to a flight of wooden steps and at the top he was faced by three doors. He knocked on one marked *FORD*, and a voice called, 'Come in!' Of course the room overlooked the ubiquitous harbour, he couldn't escape from it, not that he wanted to. It was a bedsitter, a bit threadbare and over-used, but clean and tidy. 'What do you want, love?' Millie Ford in a housecoat and mules was standing by a tiny electric stove, waiting for a saucepan of milk to heat. 'I'm making some coffee, want some?'

Wycliffe refused. She was thirtyish, plump, a bit over-ripe, but attractive. 'I'm a police officer.'

She laughed in a bored way. 'I've heard that one before, dear, but I can spot a dick a mile off. Now, what do you want? Are you after something special?'

Wycliffe flapped his warrant card and she looked at it, incredulous. 'On the level? I wouldn't have said you was big enough, they must be making 'em in the handy pocket size. A chief super, too . . .!' She pointed to the only chair in the room. 'You better sit down.' She poured the milk into a half filled cup of coffee. 'Sure you won't? Well, what have I done now?'

Wycliffe looked round the room. He'd seen hundreds like it, most of them a great deal more squalid. She had been ironing a frock and the ironing board was wedged into the little space between the bed and the window. Over the bed there was a piece of poker-work: *Bless this house!*

She caught his eye and grinned. 'I expect you know why I'm here,' he began.

She shook her mop of black hair. 'I don't, love, honest.'

He looked at her suspiciously but she seemed to be telling the truth. 'A girl was strangled at the Marina last night.'

She stopped short in the act of sipping her coffee. 'But I was . . .'

'. . . there last night, I know.'

She was shocked and scared. She put her cup down on the stove, sat on the bed and faced him. 'Was it one . . . ?'

He shook his head. 'A stranger, we don't know who she was.'

She was relieved and he didn't blame her. She brought out a packet of cigarettes from the pocket of her housecoat and looked vaguely round for matches. He gave her a box and she lit a cigarette which set her coughing.

'She was in seventeen, next door to you.'

'Ah!'

'Now I want you to tell me all you can remember about last night from the time you picked up your man.'

She blew her nose after the coughing fit and seemed to be collecting her thoughts. 'I usually do The Ship, and I was there last evening. I got into conversation with a chap and we had a few drinks although he was three parts cut before we started. When they shut at half ten he asked me to come back with him. I asked him where and he said the Marina, so that was all right. He was only a youngster and when we got out in the air he made heavy weather of it so that it took me some time to get him there and then he just flaked out on the bed. Not that I was bothered, I got into bed and tried to get some sleep . . .'

'You didn't see anybody?'

'In the Marina? Only Ernie, he was poking about in the little office when we came in and he helped me to get his lordship upstairs.'

'Well?'

She drew on her cigarette thoughtfully. 'I could hear a couple next door and I thought it must be one of ours with a client. I couldn't get off to sleep so I lay there trying to guess who it was . . . you know how you do . . .'

'What could you hear?'

'Just voices, a man and a woman talking but I couldn't hear what they were saying. I only wished they would shut up. Oh yes! – the man coughed a lot – a smoker's cough.'

'Were they quarrelling?'

'No, just talking. A lot of men pick up a girl because they want a woman to talk to – funny really.'

Wycliffe sat there staring out of the window watching the purple dusk steal over the harbour like a mist and he was happy. He was feeling the texture of another life with sympathy and understanding – these encounters were the reward, not the penalty of his work. 'Then?'

'Well, it must have been around midnight when I heard somebody come out of the room and pass my door. I thought it must be the girl going home and wished I could go too but my fellow hadn't forked out and I would have to let Ernie have his cut anyway.'

'You're sure that this was around midnight?'

'No, I couldn't be sure of the time – not really.'

'And you heard nothing more all night?'

'Oh yes I did. Probably I dozed for a bit but some time later I heard them talking again and that seemed odd. She must have come back and I couldn't understand it. This time they did seem to be quarrelling but they kept their voices low . . .'

'The same voices?'

She looked puzzled. 'Well, they must have been, mustn't they?' Wycliffe said nothing and she went on, 'Then they stopped talking and started . . .'

'What?'

'To get down to it – I mean, there's no doubt about it with those beds in the Marina.'

'Anything more?'

'No, I didn't hear any more, I must have gone off to sleep properly after that. The next thing I knew it was getting light and my chap woke up. I told him I wanted my money and after a bit he pulled out his wallet and told me to take it. He had the father and mother of a hangover and I don't think he had a clue where he was or who I was . . . Anyway I took four quid and beat it . . . After all it wasn't my fault if . . .'

Wycliffe agreed.

'To think that next door that poor girl . . .' Millie found a handkerchief and dabbed her eyes. The most poignant grief of all when one can say, 'There but for the grace of God . . .'

Wycliffe walked back to the hotel and found Helen in the lounge reading. She looked up with a welcoming smile. 'Have you had a meal?'

'What? Oh, yes thanks.' He was still in a different world from this air-conditioned lounge with its soft lights, thick carpets and silent waiters. This world was less real to him, less comprehensible; it was not that he wanted to . . . He sighed. 'I had curried stew.'

Helen laughed. 'Was it good?'

What would she say if he told her that he had been entertained by a pimp and his Jamaican tart? 'Yes, very good.'

They had a drink together, then Helen said that she felt like bed.

'I'll be with you in ten minutes.'

He lit his pipe and went out on to the terrace. He stood, his arms resting on the balustrade. The waters of the harbour, dark and mysterious, dozens of riding lights sending their quivering ribbons of yellow across its surface. Well away to the right, the docks, a blaze of light, the only sounds a low pitched hum from some machinery and the hiss of escaping steam.

One man was with the dead girl until around midnight. They talked amicably. Had this man left before another appeared on the fire escape? Was the man on the fire escape spying on the couple? It seemed probable that he had come in through the bathroom window, the official way on to the escape in an emergency. In which case the girl had unfastened the window for him. This time the talk was less friendly: 'They seemed to be quarrelling but they kept their voices low'. But this visit had ended in copulation – and in murder.

Two men? It seemed so. So far he had heard of three in the case – four if he counted Ernie Piper. The boy with the guitar, the man in the pinstripes whom Kathy had found going through the register and the chap in cap and mackintosh she had seen talking to the dead girl. Was it one of these who had spent an hour with her? And another of them who had strangled her, then battered her face beyond recognition?

CHAPTER THREE

A morning conference in the superintendent's little office.

'As I see it, the bloke came the first time to make contact, to find out if she had the money and was able to do a deal. She satisfied him and he went off to get the stuff . . .' Fehling spoke in a ponderously judicial way which was one more source of irritation to Wycliffe.

'You still think that she was buying dope?'

The inspector blew out his cheeks. 'Oh, I don't think there can be any doubt on that score, it's another matter to decide what went wrong.' He studied his finger-tips then added, 'Quite another matter.'

Wycliffe was standing looking out of the window of the office. It was as though he had to keep in touch with the world outside, a room without windows would have been torture to him. The view was uninspiring, an exercise yard and beyond a great expanse of corrugated asbestos, the wall and roof of a garage. 'What do you think, Jim?'

Chief Inspector Gill's ugly expressive features creased in dissatisfaction. 'It sounds likely enough on the face of it but according to what you've just told us they must have spent the best part of an hour together just gossiping. That hardly sounds like a preliminary session to spy out the land – more as if they were old friends. But if they knew each other so well, why didn't he bring the goods with him? In any case, why was she killed?'

Fehling took up the challenge. 'There are at least two possible explanations. When he came back with the dope it's feasible that she wasn't satisfied, or that she tried for a better deal – the girl says she heard them quarrelling.'

'So he makes love to her, strangles her, bashes her face in, then goes off without the money.'

Wycliffe's manner made Fehling flush. 'It sounds a bit thin, but you know as well as I do that you can't predict what a man will or won't do under stress.'

'You said that there were two possibilities – what was the other?'

'That they didn't quarrel about the deal but that her friend decided to round off the evening by giving her a tumble and she put up a fight.'

'So he strangled her?'

'It wouldn't be the first time!' Fehling was on the defensive.

'It couldn't have been much of a fight: Millie Ford heard nothing of it and she was next door.'

'But the girl was strangled and she did have her face battered.'

Wycliffe turned back to the window. 'Yes, and a thousand pounds was left untouched in a drawer. In any case, what about the chap on the fire escape? Where does he come into it?'

Fehling nodded. 'I've thought of that, I believe he was the same man. The front door of the hotel is fitted with a Yale-type lock which is kept clipped back but I found out from Piper that the catch is liable to slip and you find yourself locked out.'

'You think that's what happened to your friend?'

Fehling was pleased with himself. 'I do. Think of it, sir. After his first session with the girl he goes to get the stuff and when he comes back he finds the door locked. Naturally he doesn't want to rouse the house so he nips round and up the fire escape, taps on the girl's window and she lets him in through the bathroom.'

Chief Inspector Gill chuckled. 'That's very ingenious.'

Wycliffe grunted but said nothing. He hadn't a very high opinion of Fehling but he had to admit that there was some sort of case. If the girl wasn't buying dope, why would she hang around with a thousand pounds in used notes in a dockland hotel? Or had she *sold* something? He sighed. Speculation was useless until he knew who she was. 'What are you going to do next?'

Fehling felt that he had scored. 'I thought of looking into the docks angle. What ships are in? Itinerary of last trip? Who was sleeping ashore? – that sort of thing. I also planned to send out circulars – anybody in the vicinity of the Marina between, say, eleven and three.'

Wycliffe nodded. Fehling was right, whatever the reason for the crime it seemed to be linked with the docks or at least with the sea and seamen. 'I think you're on the right lines,' he said in a belated attempt to make amends.

Gill offered round a case containing thin black cheroots which were refused. He had changed to cheroots maintaining that they were less hazardous than cigarettes. He allowed himself only five a day, so that smoking one added something special to any occasion as the advertisement said that it would. Wycliffe lit his pipe in self defence. 'Yesterday evening,' Gill said, 'Inspector Fehling and I made a round of the cafés in the main street and as far as the docks. The Marina doesn't do meals other than breakfast and she must have eaten somewhere. It seems that she used a place almost by the dock gates and not above a hundred yards from the hotel. The chap who runs it had noticed an "auburn-haired dolly" whom he described "as the sort of bird to keep a man awake at night".'

'Poetic, really,' Wycliffe said. 'Was she always alone?'

'Always. The café owner was puzzled by her, she wasn't the sort he expected to get in a place like his.'

'What sort of place is it?'

Gill considered. 'It's really a lorry drivers' caf. Clean enough, friendly, but not much choice beyond the bangers and mash and a cuppa. I imagine it's used mainly by lorry drivers taking stuff in and out of the docks.'

'Not by the locals?'

Gill looked at him sharply. 'No, do you think that's why she went there?'

Wycliffe wished sometimes that Gill did not know him so well. He made an irritable movement to save a reply. He turned to Fehling. 'Why was her face battered in? That's what I want to know.'

'The chap went berserk, scared out of his wits,' Fehling said.

'Is that what you think?' Wycliffe's blank stare was turned on Gill.

The chief inspector shook his head. 'No, either her identification would lead direct to her killer or there are local associations which he doesn't want known.'

'Or both.'

'Could be.'

The telephone rang and Wycliffe answered it. 'Wycliffe.' It was the station sergeant. 'The guitarist, sir, whose photo went out on the telly last night – he's on the telephone, wants to know what it's all about.'

'Is he a local?'

'He's living in the town; he's got a flat in Marine Walk, chap by the name of Graham.'

'Tell him we'll send somebody along to talk to him – say during the next hour, then find out all you can about him from your chaps.'

'We could bring him in, sir.'

'No!' Wycliffe believed that when you brought a man into the police station you saw only half of him. He decided to interview Graham himself.

'He must be a cool one,' Gill said. 'The average man seeing his picture on the telly like that would be on to the nick before the news-reader got to the next item.'

'There aren't any average men left!' Wycliffe growled.

Before he left for Marine Walk he was briefed by the station sergeant. 'Kenneth Graham, sir, he runs a pop group and is known professionally as Kenny the Man. They seem to make a fairly plush living in the season, playing at several resorts up and down the West Country.'

Wycliffe set out.

A chief superintendent's place during a murder inquiry is usually established in the nearest police station but it can be in a village hall or even a caravan. As the officer in charge of the inquiry it is his job to remain at the centre coordinating all aspects of the investigation, receiving reports and deploying men and resources to the best advantage. The most Wycliffe had ever conceded to this official view of his duties was to telephone in at reasonable intervals or to keep in touch through his car radio. He had to get out and about, to get the smell of the chase. He had to meet witnesses in their normal surroundings. 'Field work,' he called it. He could, of course, have had his witnesses brought in. He could have carried out formal interrogations in the stultifying atmosphere of the police station where innocent people soon begin to behave like crooks. But Wycliffe believed that what he called *personal* crimes are more likely to be solved by getting to know the people involved, getting to know them so well that you begin to think as they do.

Two criticisms had been levelled at him at every stage of his career: 'He does not take well to discipline', and 'He often becomes too emotionally involved with his cases'. Damning criticisms of a policeman – Wycliffe never understood why they hadn't blocked his promotion, but he suspected that it was because the solemn Jacks who insisted on reams of paper rarely read what was on it. And he had a good reputation as a villain catcher.

Marine Walk circles the promontory which divides the harbour from the open sea. On the harbour side its low cliffs overhang the docks and on the sea side a fringe of sandy beaches, too small for exploitation, provide refuge for holidaymakers who enjoy peace and quiet. The houses are on the sea side and he drove round catching tantalizing glimpses of the sea through the trees which grow on the gentle slopes almost to the water's edge.

Graham lived in the upper flat of an Edwardian villa which had been modernized and converted into two flats with an outside staircase. The stairs ended on a glass roofed balcony with a magnificent panoramic view of the whole bay.

'Are you a copper?'

Kenny wore tight jeans and a floral shirt but he had changed his hair style since the photograph: instead of allowing it to hang lankly round his hatchet face he was now giving it the wave and set treatment.

'Chief Superintendent Wycliffe.'

'You'd better come in.'

To Wycliffe's surprise, the flat could hardly have been more conventional. Everything shone and though the taste was a bit *Coronation Street*, it had all been carefully chosen and cost money. In the lounge there was everything from a gleaming cocktail cabinet with chrome fittings to the most stupendous fake-log electric fire Wycliffe had ever seen, as well as china ducks clinging to the wall in frozen flight. Wycliffe was fascinated by the seeming incongruity of it all. 'Do you live with your parents?' It seemed the most likely explanation.

But Kenny shook his head. 'You're looking at the gear? No, it's just that I like somewhere nice to come home to and I'm not short of a few bob. As a matter of fact I share with one of my mates.' He sat on the arm of a magenta-coloured cut moquette easy chair. 'Well, what's this all about then? It don't do a chap in my position any good to be put on the telly by the police. People will think I've done something.'

Wycliffe was perched on the edge of a settee trying to stop himself falling back into its monstrous clutches. 'About the photograph, Mr Graham, is it one you use for publicity purposes?'

'No, definitely not. We're a group and we sell as a group – private enterprise is out. That's one other reason why putting me on the telly won't do me any good.'

'The girl who had this photograph was murdered.'

'Yeh?' He sounded impressed and shocked. 'Who was she?'

'That's what we want to find out and it's why we need your help.'

Kenny took a cigarette from a dispenser on one of several little tables scattered about the room. He lit it and gave his attention once more to the superintendent. 'Got a photo?'

'No.'

'Well, I can't help, can I?'

'She was twenty-one or two, auburn haired, good looking, small, and she had a mole under her left breast. People who saw her when she was alive describe her as "eye-catching".'

Kenny had stopped smoking and was looking at the superintendent with close attention. 'Tell me some more.'

'There's not much else to tell, but these are some of the things she had with her . . .' He took a small parcel from his pocket, unwrapped it and spread out the few bits of jewelry they had found in her room. 'Recognize any of it?'

Kenny picked up the garnet bracelet. 'I gave her that. She had a thing about rubies but I couldn't run to that so we settled for the next best thing.'

'So you knew her.'

Kenny nodded, his eyes staring distantly, then he sighed, 'She was a doll!'

'What was her name and when did you know her?'

At that moment the door opened and a tousle-headed brunette in a baby-doll nightie came in. She was stretching her arms and yawning. 'What time is it?' She took a cigarette and looked vaguely round the room for a light. Wycliffe might not have been there for all the notice she took. 'God! I feel awful this morning!' She saw the jewelry. 'Are they for me?'

Kenny went over and took her by the shoulders. 'Go back to bed, Chick, or get yourself dressed.' He propelled her out of the room and rounded off his instructions with a resounding slap on her rump which made her squeal. He came back looking sheepish. 'Sorry about that.'

'All part of life's rich pattern,' Wycliffe said. 'Now, you were telling me . . .'

'Dawn Peters she was called, she did a summer season at the Voodoo last year.'

'The Voodoo is a club?'

'Yes, a plush place if you go by the prices. Anyway they hire two bands for the season, one pop and one trad. We was there last year and she was one of two strippers. *The Fabulous Dawn*, they billed her and for once they were right. She used to have the old men sitting on the edges of their seats and begging. Every man in the place was convinced she was doing it for him and that included me – and I'm used to it.'

'You got to know her outside the club?'

He lit another cigarette. 'Yeh.' He was less anxious to talk now.

'Well?'

'Well enough.' He upset ash down the front of his shirt and took time off to brush it on to newspaper. 'I would have married her.'

'Did she live with you here?'

'I didn't have this place then; anyway she shared a flat with the other girl – Sadie. Sadie's still at the Voodoo, but she isn't in the same league.'

'You asked her to marry you?'

'Yeh, and she turned me down. I was lucky.'

'Lucky?'

He crushed out his cigarette in a huge plated ashtray with a press-down middle. 'That's what I said. For one thing she was married already and for another . . .' His voice trailed off. 'She was a case! She had the devil in her. It was any man any time but there was more to it than that.' He paused again, searching for words to describe something which had impressed him. 'She would always go to the limit and a bit further – you know what I mean? That sort of bird's fine to have fun with, but when it comes to the old steak and chips then you want something a bit more steady. Get me?

'It was the same in her act – I mean there are limits even for a stripper in a private club. When she turned it in at the Voodoo they lost a packet but old Quackers, the proprietor, told me himself that he was glad to see her go. With her antics on and off the stage she would have got the place shut down.'

'Where did she go when she left the Voodoo?'

Kenny shrugged. 'Up to the smoke but don't ask me where. She said she had a West End contract and she was probably telling the truth.'

'You said she was married. I take it she wasn't living with her husband?'

'I told you she was sharing with the other girl. I was new to the town then and I never knew the details but I heard gossip. Apparently she was married to some local square who took a pretty dim view of her goings on.' He grinned. 'I can't say as I blame him for that.'

Wycliffe stood up. From the window he could see the whole sweep of the bay from the lighthouse round a ten-mile stretch of coastline to the jagged teeth of the Meudon Rocks. He wondered if Kenny ever looked out of the window, or was it just another status symbol?

'Well, thank you for your help, Mr Graham. You haven't got a photograph of her, I suppose?'

Kenny shook his head. 'I never keep photos of dames, it makes for trouble, but there should be plenty at the club.'

Wycliffe moved towards the door. 'Is your group working at the moment?'

'Oh yeh, we're doing a season at the Scala.'

'Every night?'

'Except Tuesdays and Sundays. They have Bingo on Tuesdays.'

'Where were you on Tuesday night, then?'

Kenny looked shaken. 'Here! Come off it! You coppers are all alike.'

'Routine, Mr Graham, just routine. Where were you?'

He was aggrieved. 'I took the chick to that Indian place in Market Street for a nosh then we came back here early and went to bed.'

'Have you got a car?'

'Yeh. What of it?'

'Nothing. Did you know that Dawn Peters was back in the town?'

Kenny's aggressiveness increased with his nervousness. 'No, I didn't know, and if I had I wouldn't have been interested, copper!'

Wycliffe let himself out into the corridor and turned for a final word: 'Do you think Dawn Peters was her real name?'

'How the hell should I know?' Kenny the Man was disillusioned.

Wycliffe caught himself chuckling as he went down the steps, but if anybody had asked him why, he couldn't have told them. He would probably have grunted or he might have said, 'Just people.'

He drove back slowly to the centre of the town and parked on one of the quays, then he strolled in the main street. It was past one o'clock and the population of the town seemed to have its whole mind on food. It was too late to go back to the hotel for lunch but getting a meal otherwise was a competitive business and he was discouraged by the heat, by the crowded tables, by the queues and by the fact that every available potato seemed to have undergone a metamorphosis into chips. He took refuge in a pub and made a meal off ham sandwiches with mustard and a pint of beer. All round him the talk was of cricket, in which he had no interest. No-one so much as mentioned the murder. He stayed until two and followed his beer with a whisky.

'The Voodoo? They don't open till evening but you may find somebody there . . . Anyway, it's after you pass the church next to the off-licence.' Wycliffe walked once more in the sunshine while others were hurrying back to work.

The afternoon heat was oppressive, perspiration made his collar limp and his shirt stuck to his back. The Voodoo had no frontage, only a discreet entrance with a neon sign over the door, unlit. He pushed open the door and found himself at the top of a flight of carpeted stairs which led down below street level. At the bottom he was in a foyer with a cloakroom counter on his right and a couple of padded doors labelled by some retarded character *Adams* and *Eves*, respectively. Red, upholstered banquettes occupied every spare foot of wall space and above them there were framed photographs of show-business personalities, some of them well enough known to be vaguely familiar to the superintendent. Two showed an insipid looking blonde with nothing on but a head-dress and these were autographed *Sadie*. A pair of swing doors with figured glass panels opened into a very large dimly lit room with a curtained stage at one end, a central dance floor and tables and chairs disposed in two ranks on the carpeted fringe. The pervading colour was red, and the walls were hung with huge grinning masks and grotesque totems against a mural background depicting mythical monsters in vaguely erotic involvement. The stage and the bar on the far side were flanked by ten-foot-high figures which looked like refugees from Easter Island but were probably made of polystyrene. A faint smell of stale tobacco and alcohol blended with an indescribable synthetic scent out of an aerosol. But it was cool, like a cellar. There was nobody to be seen. 'Anybody about?'

After a second and a third try, a woman came down the steps from the stage. A bottle blonde, older than she tried to look; inclined to be fleshy, she looked naked rather than provocative in a psychedelic mini-dress which revealed too much white thigh. 'Who are you?'

'I want to see the owner.'

'He's not in.'

'I'm Chief Superintendent Wycliffe, Area CID.'

'What do you want?'

'I'll tell the owner when you've found him.'

She looked him over, then went back the way she had come. Wycliffe sat himself in one of the comfortable armchairs provided for the paying customers and lit his pipe. In about three minutes a man came down from the stage, forty plus, foppishly dressed in cavalry twill slacks, a modish shirt with green stripes and gold links, a green waistcoat with gilt buttons. His face was pink and rather podgy. His blue eyes looked out through rimless glasses and he spoke in an authoritative manner, intended to subdue. He was smooth, too smooth by half. 'Good afternoon, superintendent, nothing wrong, I trust?'

'I hope not, Mr . . .'

'Masson-Smythe – I'm the proprietor.' 'Quackers', Kenny the Man had called him, but not, Wycliffe was prepared to bet, to his face.

Wycliffe remained seated in his chair, smoking his pipe, Masson-Smythe stood over him, rocking on his heels. 'I am making enquiries about a Miss Dawn Peters, do you know her?'

The proprietor straightened the cuffs of his shirt, displaying the gold links. 'We had a cabaret artiste of that name who worked here last season.'

'A stripper?'

Masson-Smythe raised his eyebrows in disapproval. 'She was a speciality dancer and her act possessed great artistic merit.'

'I'm sure it did. She's been murdered.'

The eyes behind the spectacles widened.

'Was Dawn Peters her real name?'

'It was the name she used in her dealings with me.'

Wycliffe's manner hardened. 'But you employed her! What about insurance, income tax, S.E.T.?'

Masson-Smythe was curt. 'All our artistes have contracts, they are self-employed.'

'Was she good at her job?'

'She attracted patrons.'

There was something about Masson-Smythe's face which had been troubling the superintendent, now he realized what it was. Words came from his lips as from a ventriloquist's doll; there was scarcely any change of expression. 'You must have had photographs of her for display purposes?'

'Certainly.'

'I would like to see them.'

For some reason this seemed to touch a tender spot and the man lost something of his aggressive self-assurance. Wycliffe noticed little beads of perspiration on his upper lip. Something to hide. 'I'm sorry, we do not keep photographs of artistes who are no longer under contract with us, the rapid turnover in the entertainment business makes it . . .'

Wycliffe mentioned two or three names off the photographs in the foyer. 'Are these people under contract with you at present?'

'They are in quite a different category, superintendent, they are celebrities and the fact that they have performed here in the past is, itself, an advertisement.'

Wycliffe smoked placidly and Masson-Smythe continued to stand over him. 'I would like to know on what date Dawn Peters started to work here and under what circumstances she was offered a contract.'

For a moment it seemed that the man might refuse but after some hesitation he shrugged and said, 'Then we'd better move to my office.'

His office was on the street level but at the back of the building. It could have been the office of a prosperous accountant, and it occurred to Wycliffe that Masson-Smythe himself looked more like an accountant than a night club owner. He went to a filing cabinet, unlocked it, and drew out a file. He seated himself in an upholstered swivel chair behind his desk and waved Wycliffe to one of the client's chairs. 'Her contract is dated May tenth, and was to run for four months. I have a note here that I interviewed her first on the twenty-second of April.'

'Was she recommended to you?'

Masson-Smythe spread the papers on his desk and pretended to consult them. 'No, she turned up at a rehearsal and asked for a job. At first I didn't take her seriously; too many girls down on their luck think all they have to do is to take off their clothes in public to make their fortunes. It is not as simple as that.'

'Did she appear to be down on her luck?'

He considered. 'No, she was well dressed and well groomed, but she said that she needed money. I asked her if she had had any experience of cabaret work and she said that she had not. I was on the point of sending her away but there was something about her . . . She was an extremely attractive girl but in this business that isn't enough – a girl needs a certain personality and I thought that she might have it.'

'You gave her an audition?' (Do you audition a stripper?)

'There and then.' He took a cigarette from a box on his desk and lit it. 'She was a natural. It is not an easy thing, even for an experienced girl, to give a good performance under rehearsal conditions – no lights, no audience, no glamour, but despite all that she managed to make her performance intimate and provocative.'

'Yet you were not sorry when her contract ended?'

The blue eyes behind the glasses were cold. 'Indeed?'

Wycliffe fixed him with a bland stare. 'I have been told that you were glad to be rid of her, is that true or not?'

'Perfectly true!' It was the woman Wycliffe had seen downstairs. She came in and stood by Masson-Smythe's chair.

'My wife, Thelma, superintendent. I think that you have already met.'

After the civilities, he went on, 'The superintendent is making enquiries about Dawn Peters . . . Apparently she has been murdered.' No news to the little wife who had obviously been listening outside the door.

Wycliffe turned to her. 'You agree that you and your husband were glad to see her go – why?'

'She was a whore and this place is not a brothel. Does that answer your question?'

Masson-Smythe flushed but said nothing. His wife still stood by him, one hand on his chair as though asserting possession. A formidable woman, Wycliffe thought. Seen in a good light, the hard line of her jaw, a mean little mouth and slightly protuberant eyes disposed of what appeal she seemed to have in the dim light downstairs. Wycliffe knew the sort: hard with men, vicious with other women. Some of them had found their true vocations in the Nazi women's gaols.

'She persisted in dating the patrons which, of course, is strictly against the rules.'

And not only the patrons, Wycliffe thought. Hubby had probably taken a turn with the rest.

'When did she leave the Voodoo?'

Masson-Smythe glanced uneasily at his wife then referred to his papers. 'On August twenty-eighth.'

'Before her contract expired?'

'My husband was forced to terminate it.'

'Do you know where she went after she left?'

'I'm afraid her plans had no interest for us.'

Wycliffe took out his notebook and opened it. 'The other girl who worked with you last season is still with you, I should like her name and address.'

'Sadie Field, 4a, Mount Zion, but she can tell you nothing you don't know already.'

Thelma laughed. 'The original dumb blonde – that's Sadie.'

Wycliffe wrote down the address, put away his notebook and stood up. Thelma came out from behind the desk. 'One question, superintendent, was it Dawn Peters who was found strangled in a hotel bedroom?'

'It seems so.'

'I read about it in the papers.'

'Yes.'

Wycliffe had nothing against these people but he wished like hell he had. With most of the people he met, even the bent ones, it was all too easy to discover the common bond of their humanity, but not with this couple. Perhaps they had never been and never would be in trouble with the law but they repelled him. Mean. They lacked charity. St Paul said, 'Though I speak with the tongues of men and of angels and have not charity, I am become as a sounding brass or a tinkling cymbal.' Wycliffe thought so too.

The club owner came with him to the foyer and watched him as he walked up the stairs. As Wycliffe opened the street door he almost collided with a man coming in. A small dark chap with heavily lined features, shabbily dressed. Wycliffe had known plenty like him as bookie's runners before the new laws and he would probably never have given the incident another thought had it not been for the man's obvious nervousness. Before closing the door Wycliffe glanced down the stairs at Masson-Smythe who seemed anything but glad to see his visitor.

Outside the heat reflected from the pavements was like a blast from a baker's oven.

CHAPTER FOUR

Mount Zion, where Sadie lived, was a narrow, steep lane off the main street. It was so steep that there were steps at intervals and a rail running down the middle. Her flat comprised only two rooms and a share in the usual offices of an old tenement building which had been more or less modernized. It was on the second floor and overlooked a concrete yard festooned with washing. The living room, which had a curtained alcove for a kitchen, was furnished with a studio couch, a couple of easy chairs in faded chintz covers, a scratched dining table and two high-backed dining chairs, 1930 vintage. Evidently Sadie was dumb enough to be cheap.

'Miss Sadie Field?' Wycliffe introduced himself.

Sadie looked scared. She had a delicate prettiness, fair hair and freckles, and her figure was of the kind called 'trim', nothing exotic, certainly nothing erotic about her. When the patrons of the Voodoo watched Sadie take off her clothes they must have imagined themselves to be spying on the girl next door. She pulled her housecoat round her and retied the sash. 'Isn't it hot?'

'You were a friend of Dawn Peters?'

Nervous. 'We used to share this flat. Is there something wrong?'

He encouraged her to sit and took a seat beside her on the couch. He had to shift a copy of the *Daily Mirror* and a paperback with a picture on the cover of a Dr Kildare character in gentlemanly embrace with a pretty nurse. A report on the finding of the body had a two-column spread at the foot of the front page of the *Mirror*. He pointed to it. 'Have you read this?'

'Yes.' Wide-eyed. She was gripping her hands together so tightly that the knuckles whitened. 'Was it her?'

'I'm afraid so.'

She looked as though she was going to cry but didn't.

'We know almost nothing about her and we need your help.'

She was staring out of the open window at the silhouettes of the buildings across the court. Between them you could glimpse the tops of the masts of craft in the harbour. 'I don't know much about her before she came to live with me and I haven't heard from her since she left . . .'

'When did she come here? Was it when she started to work at the club?'

She shook her head. 'Before. It was nearly two years ago – late August or early September.' She grinned. 'We met in the launderette, we got talking and she asked me if I knew of any cheap lodgings. The girl who shared with me had left so I brought her back. She liked it and stayed.'

'Did you know that she was married?'

'I didn't when she came here first, but people told me soon enough.'

'She didn't tell you herself?'

'Not till she'd been here a good while.'

'I understand that she was married to a local man?'

Sadie nodded. 'A man called Collins, he owns the bookshop. He's a lot older.'

'So that her real name wasn't Peters.'

'No, she wasn't called Dawn, either, her name was Julie.'

Julie Collins.

'I suppose you suggested that she should try for a job at the club?'

She looked surprised. 'No, I had no idea that she was even thinking of it until she turned up one afternoon at a rehearsal and Mr Masson-Smythe gave her an audition. She was like that – kept things to herself.'

'She lived here for eight or nine months before she started work at the club?'

'About that.'

'What did she live on?'

The translucent skin of her forehead wrinkled. 'She had money. It might not have been much but it was enough to live on. And she went with men though I don't know whether they paid her.'

A statement of fact with no overtones of comment but he felt suddenly irritated. Would nobody tell him what he wanted to know about this girl? She must have done most of the same things as other people, and some different, but all he could learn of her was that she went with men. 'Did she go out much?'

'Not much. For days at a time she wouldn't put a foot outside the door.'

'What did she do all day?'

Sadie picked at a loose thread in the chintz cover. 'She used to read a lot.'

'What did she read?' Probably a useless question.

She spread her hands in a little helpless gesture. 'Books from the library and she used to buy books sometimes.'

Wycliffe stood up and started to wander round the room. He was restless. Here he had his first chance to make some real contact with the dead girl. She had lived in these rooms for more than ten months. There must be something! He reached the door of the bedroom and pushed it open, Sadie close on his heels. 'It's not very tidy!' It wasn't, but neither was it dirty or squalid. Two single beds with nondescript coverlets, an old-fashioned dressing table with triple mirrors, a wardrobe with a front mirror and a grotesquely fretted top, a couple of wicker chairs littered with underwear. In an alcove there were shelves and on one of them books. 'Are these hers?' Hopeful.

'What? Oh yes, she left them behind.'

The random fall-out from almost any library: two or three book club selections, Durrell's *Justine*, a couple of Maigrets, a Nicolas Freeling, Dostoevsky's *Possessed* . . . the Collected Poems of Dylan Thomas, *Ulysses* . . . *Ulysses* had an inscription on the fly-leaf:

'To my love.
'Can men more injure women than to say
They love them for that, by which they are not they?
W.'

More ways than one of taking that. In any case it was an odd thing to quote to your girl friend. But literary. The other books were older and had passed through one or more secondhand shops, their decline recorded in pencilled prices on their fly-leaves. Several were books of poetry, Burns, Shelley, Keats . . . the rest were novels, *Wuthering Heights, Tess of the d'Urbervilles, Ann Veronica* . . .

A literary whore? Why not? Wycliffe was broadminded and had never believed in demarcation. And surely the tapestry of history must be the richer for its cultured courtesans?

He turned away from the books. 'You still share?'

'A staff supervisor from Wandell's.'

'Dawn . . . Julie, didn't tell you much about herself?'

She stood beside him, nervous, anxious to please. 'Not much, she didn't talk much about anything.'

'Have you got a photograph of her?'

'No, but there must be plenty at the club.'

'You got on with her? I mean, was she easy to live with?'

A small frown as she spotted and dived for a pair of tights lying on the floor. She picked them up and stuffed them under a cushion. 'Oh, yes.'

'No quarrels?'

A faint flush. 'Not quarrels . . .'

'Differences then – what about?'

'Several times she brought men home and I didn't like that so in the end I stopped it.'

'Apart from these men, did anybody ever come to see her?'

'Nobody.'

He caught the momentary hesitation in her manner. 'Sure?'

She sat on the edge of her bed and swept back her hair with the unselfconscious grace of a little girl. 'I don't know. One afternoon as I was coming up the stairs I saw a man coming out of our flat. It was just after I'd told her I wouldn't have men . . . Anyway, when I got in I asked her who the man was and she pretended there hadn't been anybody. I called her a liar and after a minute or two she said, "If you must know, that was my husband, he's been trying to persuade me to come back to him".'

'You believed her?'

'I don't know, I think so.'

'When was this?'

'Not long before she finished at the club and went off to London.'

'Surely you must know this man Collins?'

'Not really, I've seen him once or twice but the stairs are very dark – it could have been him.'

'Did she tell you anything about her husband?'

'Not really. I remember I said, "Why did you leave

him?" and she said, "He needed a mother not a wife; he didn't know what it was all about".'

'Perhaps he failed to love her for that by which she was not he.'

'What's that?' She looked at him sharply.

'Just thinking aloud.'

He wandered back into the living room and Sadie followed, watching his every move, puzzled by this strange man who was nothing like any policeman she had known. His questions, when they came, seemed almost incidental to some deeper preoccupation. And this was so: his mind was a turmoil of impressions, ideas, recollections, without pattern or purpose. At such times he seemed to lose his judgement, every fact seemed to carry the same weight, every possibility to be equally credible. Once, this state of mind had bothered him, he had supposed that his job demanded crisp, incisive logic; only when he found, to his surprise, that he was looked upon as successful, did he slowly acquire confidence to stifle his misgivings. Now, he rationalized his muddled thinking, saying that ideas crystallized from it.

The curtains of the kitchen alcove were drawn back and he found himself staring out through the little window above the sink. It gave a view of a cluster of mellow slate roofs which had changed little in a century and a half. They climbed steeply to a rising mound until, not far away, they cut the skyline in bold, jagged thrusts.

'Did she smoke?'

'Julie? A little, five or six a day, like me.'

There were so many possibilities. A slut sprawled on the couch all day, not bothering to dress until she put on her war paint to go to the club or to search for a man. Reading Dostoevsky.

'Drink?'

'Not more than you have to in our sort of job. I mean, we have to act as hostesses as well . . .'

Idly he opened the doors of one or two cupboards, a few utensils, a few groceries. A tiny refrigerator under the draining board, he stooped to open it. Half a small chicken, a bottle of milk and three or four bottles of Coca-Cola. He couldn't focus an image.

'The waiters know and whatever they bring is always watered down unless we ask for different.' She didn't seem to mind him poking about but she was puzzled by it.

'Was she sacked?'

'From the club? – No.'

'She left before her contract expired.'

'Because she wanted to.'

'That's not what they told me at the club.'

'You've been talking to Thelma, she hated her.'

'Because Julie went to bed with her husband?'

She frowned. 'That might have been part of it but they were at daggers drawn apart from that. Thelma is inclined to throw her weight about and Julie wasn't the sort to be put on.'

'They told me her contract was terminated because she dated patrons of the club.'

'Oh.'

For the first time she was holding out on him, her face resolutely closed.

Wycliffe sighed. 'She's been murdered. A man made love to her, then strangled her.'

She turned away quickly, her hand to her throat.

'We've got to find who did it – you agree?'

She still did not face him but she said, 'Yes.'

'All right! She broke one of the terms of her contract, Masson-Smythe says he sacked her for it, you say not . . .'

She faced him now, her face once more composed and frank. 'I think they wanted to get rid of her but they didn't dare.'

'Why not?'

'I think that she knew something about them – something which could have got them into serious trouble.'

'What?'

'I don't know. All I know is what happened one Monday afternoon – we have rehearsals then and this time it was the final one for a completely new show so everybody was on their toes. We had lights, costumes, everything, just like a real show. Dawn – Julie, had a new routine like the rest, this time she came on as a Firebird, dressed in dozens of chiffon scarves, all the colours of flame. She had to do a bit of ballet dancing in flickering red and orange lights as she got rid of the scarves and she did it very well. In the end of course she was naked and when she stood in the spot everybody gave her a hand – everybody except Thelma, that is.'

'She comes to rehearsals?'

'Thelma? She produces. She says she was once a Windmill girl and she seems to think that makes her an authority. Not but what she hasn't got some very good ideas.' Sadie was nothing if not fair. 'Anyway, when Julie finished her act, she said, "Well, dear, you aren't exactly a ballerina but I suppose it will have to do!" Julie didn't say anything, it wasn't easy to make her mad and Thelma went on, "After all, it isn't your dancing they come to see, is it?" Julie still said nothing and it would have passed off but when we were back in our dressing room – we shared – Thelma comes in. I could see she was up to something from the look on her face. She went straight up to Julie and said, "I didn't want to embarrass you in front of the others but I think you should have a bath before you do your act. Your legs, my dear – it shows under the lights".'

Sadie paused and moistened her lips like a little girl telling a story. 'Julie was sitting in front of the mirror brushing her hair and I could see her face in the glass. She went white then she turned round and looking up at Thelma she said, "You're doing your best to provoke me but it would be a big mistake. I know enough to put you and lover-boy out of harm's way for a very long time." You would have thought Julie had hit her. She never said another word, just stood there, then she walked out. But from then on there was never a criticism of anything Julie did, not so much as a sly dig.'

'You didn't discover what it was all about?'

'No. When she went out I asked Julie but she was quite rude. "Whatever it was about, Cheesy," she said, "it's nothing to do with you. It's better you don't know".'

'Cheesy?'

'That's what they call me, it's short for Cheesecake.' She seemed pleased to tell him.

'When did this happen? Was it shortly before she left?'

'Not long after she started to work at the club, perhaps four or five weeks.'

He made a move to go then hesitated. 'Did you like her?'

'Like her?' She echoed the words, stalling for time. 'She was easy to live with – I mean she wasn't catty like a lot of girls . . . in some ways she was quite kind.'

'But?'

Sadie searched painfully for words. 'She frightened me, I didn't understand her – she was *wild*.'

'Wild?'

'Reckless – always doing things just for kicks. You never knew what it would be next.'

'What sort of thing?'

She looked at him nervously then away again. 'She's dead now, so it can't hurt her. When she first came here we used to go shopping together and suddenly, in one of the shops, she would say, "We're going to have this on the house, Cheesy!" and she would nick something really valuable – not because she wanted it, either.'

Wycliffe nodded his understanding.

'It used to scare me rigid! But she was never happy unless she was taking risks . . .'

Food for thought, quite a lot of it; more might mean indigestion. 'You've been very helpful, Miss Field, I'm grateful and I may have to come back again.'

She had unwound during the time he had been there, now she was taut and nervous again. 'You won't say anything at the club? I can't afford to lose my job . . .'

'I'll be the soul of discretion.'

Four o'clock and the town shimmering in the heat. Over the sea, a canopy of purplish-black cloud slowly creeping up the sky like a giant shutter excluding the sunlight. He drove back to the station and as he got out of the car he felt a sudden chill with the sky darkening overhead. A moment later, a flicker of lightning and an explosive thunder clap heralding the rain. It came hissing and sweeping across the square like a wall of water as he hurried inside.

Fehling was in the HQ room typing his report, Gill was there too, his chair tilted back, his feet on the table, drinking tea. The lights were on because of the storm.

'The Deputy Chief has been asking for you.'

'Here?'

'On the blower. He wants you to ring him back at his home number.'

'What does he want?'

Gill lowered his feet to the floor. 'That's a moot point

at the moment, sir. Something with blood in it, I should think, preferably yours.'

Wycliffe poured himself a cup of cold tea. 'Well, what's new?'

'Not much. Fingerprints have matched one of the sets of dabs on your photograph of the guitar player and we've got the gen from Criminal Records.'

'Well?'

'A small-time crook who stepped out of line and tried for the big league. With four others he was concerned in a wages snatch – thirty thousand quid. They held up a security van in Battersea, the others got away but Allen was coshed by one of the security men and he got nicked.'

'Where is he now?'

Gill smiled. 'That's the point – he skipped while he was waiting to go up the steps – literally. He was below stairs in the Magistrates' Court waiting to be brought up and somehow he managed to get away. Nobody seems to know quite how but I gather there are some red faces.'

'It was all in the Crime Report a fortnight back,' Fehling volunteered.

'Was it.' Not a question, a mild snub. 'What do we know about this Allen?'

Gill picked up a typewritten sheet. 'Frederick Charles Allen, 27, five feet nine, one hundred and ninety pounds . . . blah blah . . . No fixed address . . . Approved School . . . Borstal at eighteen . . . six months housebreaking and assault in '61, two years for robbery in '64 . . . three months and six months for possession and trafficking in '66. There's a photograph.' Gill pushed over the information sheet with an attached photograph – a full-face and a profile. A square-faced young man with puffy unhealthy cheeks, deep-set eyes, a weak mouth and a low forehead, a mop of dark hair.

'He's still on the run?'

'Seems like it. Of course he could have got his mitts on that guitar player's photograph anywhere, there's nothing to say that he's in our manor.'

'There's nothing to say he isn't!' Wycliffe snapped. 'Is there any mention of a girl friend?'

'According to the notes he's a bit of a lad with the birds but no special one.'

They were interrupted by the most brilliant flash of lightning yet and a simultaneous clap of thunder which shook the building. The lights flickered but recovered. Wycliffe pointed to the photograph of Allen. 'Have you shown this to Piper at the Marina?'

'It's only just arrived. The chap I spoke to at the Yard was a bit toffee nosed but from what I could gather they're puzzled about Allen. This snatch was way out of his class.'

Wycliffe grunted. He was impatient, irritable, with the uncomfortable feeling that he was being side-tracked. 'Ask them to let us have all they can get on him.'

Then he told them about his own day. 'The Voodoo is being used as a cover for something and the girl found out about it. Admittedly that was months ago but it may still be the reason she was killed.' He turned to Fehling. 'I want you to put a round-the-clock watch on the club, but discretion above everything. If one of your flatfoots gives himself away . . .!' He made a dramatic gesture. 'And find out what you can about the Masson-Smythes, whether they've got any form, but I don't want the birds frightened off their nest. You'd better tell your fellows also to keep a special eye for Allen, if he puts in an appearance there it would mean something though I'm damned if I know what! The question is, what are they up to? What did the girl find out?'

'Trafficking. It's obvious!' from Fehling. 'Ties up with the money and with this chap Allen, he was done for possession and trafficking.'

Wycliffe took out his pouch and began to fill his pipe. 'I'll say one thing for you, you don't give up, but you may be right. It's possible that the girl bought herself into the racket as the price of her silence.'

'A dangerous thing to do, as we all know,' Gill said. He got out his cheroots and went through the ritual of lighting one. 'There are signs that cannabis is slipping through the south-western ports and that the traffic is getting organized with a distribution set-up in the area. Perhaps we've hit on it.'

Fehling drew the plastic cover over his typewriter and patted it like a pet dog. 'I'm sure of it.'

Wycliffe smoked in silence for a while. 'The resin would probably sell on the market for two-fifty a pound. What would they pay at the port?'

Gill shrugged. 'Say twenty-five to thirty.'

'So a thousand pounds should buy somewhere in the region of thirty-five or forty pounds – a tidy weight for a girl on her own.'

'We don't know that she would have been on her own, she said she was expecting her husband.' – Fehling, anxious to sustain his advantage.

'Why was she killed?'

'Probably because she was a thorn in the flesh of the Voodoo crowd.'

'Why was she battered after death?'

'I think you're making too much of that, sir.' Fehling, getting venturesome.

Wycliffe shook his head. 'If she was working for them would they kill her and leave her in possession of a thousand pounds of their money? In any case, does it *look* like the sort of killing you get when rogues fall out?' He stood up and walked to one of the windows of the long room. He stood there, his hands on the sill, his pipe clenched in his teeth, looking down on the square. The rain had stopped, the clouds were thinning and people were on the move again. He got a kick from the fact that nature could still bring the ant-hill to a stop. 'It's possible that you are right, she may have been mixed up in a small time dope ring but that wasn't why she was killed. She was killed in a moment of passion, incidentally, perhaps almost accidentally . . .'

Sardonic grin from Gill. 'Incidental death by accident – that's a new one for the book.'

Wycliffe turned to face them. 'You're getting cheeky, my lad! Anything else?'

Fehling picked up the sheet he had been typing between finger and enormous spatulate thumb. It was a wonder he didn't hit three keys at once when he typed. 'She arrived in town on Sunday night by Royal Blue coach.'

'From London?'

'She took her ticket and boarded the bus at Victoria Coach Station. The driver remembers her because she was "so small and pretty". She got off the coach in the park here and while he was getting her luggage from the boot she said, "I have to get to the Marina, do you think I'll be able to pick up a taxi?" The driver got her a taxi and saw her into it.'

'There are times when I wish I was small and pretty,' Gill said. He watched a chance smoke ring rise from his cheroot, spread and vanish. 'Do you think we've got enough to start leaning on these Masson-Smythes?'

Wycliffe was definite. 'No! For the present we just watch.'

'What about the husband – the girl's husband – Collins, I think you said?'

'I don't know, I haven't seen him.'

Gill and Fehling looked at him in surprise. Gill said, 'You want one of us . . .?'

'No.' He glanced at the clock. 'The shop will be shut in a few minutes anyway.'

Fehling was on the point of asking what that had to do with it when a warning glance from Gill stopped him. Wycliffe added, as though in self justification, 'The girl's body was only found yesterday morning, it's not as though she'd been dead a month!'

He would have found it impossible to explain his thinking. He could hardly claim that it was logical. All he knew was that underneath his apparent acceptance of what Fehling and Gill had said, hc didn't believe a word of it. He was certain that as yet they did not know what the case was about; they had been sidetracked. He knew of old that lift of the spirit which comes when you have one end of the thread in your hand. Suddenly there is a feeling of certainty. You *know*. He was a long way from that! But until then it was necessary to walk softly, to put out antennae, to get the feel and the smell of things. He would never do that if he gathered facts too quickly, there must be time to digest. He said, as though he still required to excuse himself, 'I'll see Collins in the morning. Meantime, Jim, I want you to do some snooping round the docks.'

'To find what, sir?' Gill thought it was best to get his brief clear.

'How the hell should I know? Just snoop.'

'I've been into that angle pretty thoroughly, sir.' Fehling was piqued.

'There's no reason why the chief inspector shouldn't go there himself, is there?' Fehling sighed, audibly, and Wycliffe went on, 'You know the score, Jim. One of the local lads must have a snout inside.'

'I think I get the message.'

'Good!' He envied Gill this job; loitering round the docks, hobnobbing with the men, snooping round the ships, having the odd drink with a hospitable skipper . . . You make a hell of a sacrifice for promotion. 'Have a chat with one or two of the blokes who tend on the ships; you see them lounging about the quay with their tongues hanging out so it shouldn't be too difficult or too expensive . . . And Jim! see if you come across a little dark chap with heavily lined features . . . fortyish – a little rat of a man. Reminds you of a bookie's runner. May have been a seaman, perhaps he still is.'

Gill's raised eyebrows forced him to go on, 'I saw a chap answering that description going into the Voodoo this afternoon, and I don't think Masson-Smythe was too pleased to see him.'

He was on the point of leaving when he remembered the Deputy Chief. He went into his temporary office, picked up the telephone and asked to be put through.

Deputy Chief Constable Bellings was an administrator, possibly a good one, Wycliffe was no judge, but he knew that Bellings could never have been a real policeman. No doubt he had once hammered a beat, no doubt he had done his share of CID work at the dirty end, house to house, drinking with snouts, hanging round warehouses, sleazy hotels and railway stations, questioning pimps, tarts, tearaways and, later, villains in the big time . . . But for Bellings this had been solely a means to an end, the distasteful and hazardous way to the top. Now he was nearly there, he had reached the stage where you could be objective about the disturbing variety of human weakness and wickedness which we call crime. He could smooth it all into a statistical curve and make it a matter of accounting. No wonder he disliked pegs which refused to stay in their proper holes.

'Mr Bellings? Wycliffe here, sir. I understand that you wish to speak to me.'

'To be accurate, I wished to locate you.'

'This is my HQ for the inquiry, sir.'

'I am delighted to hear it. I hope that it will be possible to contact you there. Good night, Charles!'

'Good night, sir!' And the same to you with embellishments!

He passed through the HQ room on his way out. 'I'm off!'

Fehling looked after him, mystified. 'He's cheered up! I thought he was in for a bollocking.'

'It takes him that way,' Gill said.

CHAPTER FIVE

Wycliffe and his wife stood side by side, arms resting on the balustrade, watching the harbour. The rain had gone leaving a fresh clean smell behind, everything looking sharp and incisive. The sun had set behind them but the sky was still a pale washed-out blue with smoky grey wisps of cloud tinged with gold. Out on the water a radio played a nostalgic waltz tune; further along the terrace a honeymoon couple stood close, arms round each other. Wycliffe rested his hand on his wife's. Twenty-four years ago, almost to the day, he had been a beat copper, standing on the pavement, watching people coming out of a cinema. A pretty fair girl hurried down the steps and dived past him in the direction of the bus stop. She wore an oatmeal summer coat and a saucy brown beret. And that might easily have been that, for the bus swept past and pulled in at the stop. But with only a few yards to go, she tripped and fell, badly ricking her ankle. He had rendered first aid. Helen Wills, typist; Charlie Wycliffe, copper. They had come a long way since then but for a long time the words, 'When I'm a sergeant', had seemed to be the Open Sesame to gracious living. 'We'll be able to afford a little car . . . ' Now he was a Detective Chief Superintendent and they stayed at four star hotels as a matter of course – or almost.

'A penny for them?'

'I was thinking what a smug bourgeois couple we've become.'

'Do you mind very much?'

'I don't know. I like to think I do.'

Somewhere a clock began to strike the hour. They counted though they knew the time. 'Nine o'clock.'

'Will Detective Chief Superintendent Wycliffe kindly come to reception?' A pause, then the message repeated by the young lady with a plum in her mouth, over the hotel loudspeaker system. 'Thank you!' Click! The voice had come faintly through the open windows of the lounge. Wycliffe went in obediently, stared at by the guests. Television should have convinced them that detectives don't have handcuffs hanging out of their pockets, or two heads. The girl in reception pointed to one of the telephone booths.

'Gill here, sir. I thought I'd better tell you that Ernie Piper at the Marina recognized Allen's photo. He's been staying there since Sunday in the name of Rawlings. Room twenty-one. He's one of those on Fehling's list supposed to be waiting for a ship and he's got a merchant seaman's book.'

'You've brought him in?'

Perceptible pause. ''Fraid not, he's skipped.'

Wycliffe's reply drew the attention of the girl in reception.

'He didn't sleep in his room last night. Piper had spotted him as an ex-con but he says he had no reason to think that he was a wanted man. Reasonable enough if you believe . . . '

Wycliffe did not try too hard to sound reasonable in return. 'If Piper could spot him what's wrong with the wall-eyed cretin who questioned him? What's Fehling playing at?'

'I don't think you can blame Fehling . . . '

'You must be joking! Anyway the thing is, what to do? It's too late to set up road checks, he's had twenty-four hours.' He hesitated. 'You'd better get on to the Met, they'll want to amend their circular – and Jimmy, get on to our own boys and stir them up a bit – make the fur fly.'

He was nothing like as sore as he sounded; he rarely was. Early in his career he had realized that you have to put on a show. A reputation for bloody-mindedness which doesn't go too deep is an asset. Actually he was not displeased with the turn of events; something happening in a case is better than nothing, it gives you the chance to take a fresh hold.

'I have to go out, dear.'

'Will you be late?'

'I don't know but don't wait up for me.'

'The story of my life.'

He was going to take the car but, on an impulse, decided to walk. No point in rushing around. It was getting dark, the street lamps were on but the air was soft and balmy. Girls in their summer dresses without coats, young men in shirt sleeves. They paraded through the town and through the dusk in mixed groups, effervescent, noisy, predatory; looking for trouble. Most of them were restrained from making it by a flimsy barrier of convention. On that barrier, getting thinner every year, order and security depend. The educationalists ride their bandwagons, some of them doing the splits on two at once as an insurance. Some day, somebody will knock their heads together and tell them that education is about living. Meanwhile it's your job to seal the cracks, copper!

Beyond the main street he followed the road round the harbour to the Marina. A light high in one of the attics. Kathy's room? Or was she too parading the streets? He hoped so for her sake, anything is better than loneliness when you are young.

The vestibule of the Marina was dimly lit by a fly-blown bulb over the reception desk. Piper was there in his shirt sleeves, entering figures in a cash book. One of Gill's men was half asleep in a wicker chair by a dusty potted palm. He sprang up and tried to look efficient. 'Mr Gill left word that he will be at the station, sir.'

Wycliffe went straight for Piper. 'Where has he gone?'

Piper pulled the lobe of his ear. 'I haven't a clue, super, straight up I haven't! All I know is the bastard skipped without paying his bill.'

'Did he have any contact with the girl while he was here?'

'Not to my knowledge. I've never seen 'em together but you know how it is.'

'Did he go out much?'

A bit more ear pulling. 'Come to think of it I never saw him go out at all. I only ever saw him at breakfast and he was late for that.'

'What about his other meals?'

Piper shrugged. 'I suppose he must have gone out same as the rest.'

Wycliffe rested his arms on the desk and stared at the potbellied little man, compelling his reluctant gaze. Piper shook his head. 'It's no good leaning on me, Mr Wycliffe, I don't even know what all this is about. What's he done? He never murdered the kid, did he?'

Wycliffe straightened up. 'Where's Kathy?'

Piper brightened perceptibly. 'Probably in her room, I'll get her.'

'Don't bother! I'll find it.' He made for the stairs. What would Piper have thought, or Gill, if they knew that out of simple curiosity he wanted to see Kathy's room?

The attic passage was covered with lino instead of threadbare carpet and seemed cleaner because of it. There was only one room with a light under the door and he could hear the muffled sound of a transistor radio.

He knocked. The radio clicked off. 'Who is it?' Kathy opened the door and invited him in.

He was not disappointed. She had impressed herself on the little room. The sloping boarded ceiling was half covered with photographs of pop stars, there was a shelf with a few books, an ancient record player, a table, a chair and a bed with a bright orange coverlet. The sash window was wide open, the radio stood on the sill, and she had obviously been sitting by it sewing, for an embryonic garment lay, a little heap of green silky material, on the chair, needle and cotton stabbed into it. She cleared the chair and made him sit down, perching herself on the bed, knees together, dress pulled down. 'You have come about Mr Rawlings?'

'His real name is Allen and he is wanted by the police.'

'I am sorry, he seemed a harmless man.'

'You liked him?'

'I was sorry for him.'

Sitting by the open window he seemed to be almost on top of the docks; although it was night, clanking and hissing and a massive underlying throbbing filled the room. The superstructure of one ship, a pyramid of lights, seemed only a stone's throw away. 'Doesn't the noise keep you awake?'

'I'm used to it. It did at first.'

'Why were you sorry for him?'

'He was ill, always coughing. Although he was such a big man I do not think he is very strong, he must have something wrong with his lungs.'

'Did he go out much?'

She lowered her eyes. 'He did not go out, he spend most of his time in bed reading.'

'How did he manage for food?'

'He go down for breakfast but I bring him the rest. If not I think he would have gone without.'

'You brought him food; did Ernie know?'

She shrugged. 'Ernie!' Gentle, good-natured contempt.

Wycliffe regarded the solemn face, serene, composed. He wondered from what inner strength she derived her composure. The young need a sense of security! The answer to that seemed to be a raspberry. You were forced to blame it on the generation gap and give up trying to understand. 'Did he make a pass at you?'

'No, it wasn't like that.'

'Did he tell you anything about himself?'

'Only that he was waiting for his ship and he was afraid he would not be well enough to join her. He asked me not to talk about him for if the ship people hear he is ill they will not take him.'

'Did you ever see him with the girl who was killed?'

The question seemed to surprise her. 'But he never left his room except . . . '

'Let's take a look at his room.'

Room 21 was on the same floor as the dead girl's but in the main part of the house facing the front, a narrow room over a passage on the floor below. 'Is this how he left it?'

'Just as he leave it, I only pull back the curtains.'

Which meant that he had probably waited until after dark before leaving. It might help though he hadn't much hope. The room stank of eucalyptus, a smell which always revolted him. He looked round, pulling open the drawers of a rickety chest. Two or three sexy paperbacks, a dirty handkerchief. He turned to the tin which served as a wastepaper-basket. Three empty cigarette packets, dead matches and ash, an evening newspaper and part of a sheet of stiff paper, torn raggedly. On one side, the address of the hotel written in pencil, a feminine hand, on the other, at the torn edge, half – the lower half – of a scrawled signature, and below that, typewritten: *per pro Summit Theatrical Costumiers Ltd.*

A slender link but it might mean something. He fished out a plastic envelope and slipped it in. If Thelma Masson-Smythe had written that address – then . . . Then what? He could have pushed his reasoning powers a bit further but that had never been his way. Let it all mill around. He went to the window and looked out; the same view as from Kathy's room but a floor lower. He noticed a long low building on the other side of the road almost by the dock gates. A blue neon sign read: *SNACKS & CAFÉ*.

'Is that the place where she had her meals?'

'I think so, it is where most of our people go, but of course it is always men.'

'You wouldn't think it worth their while to stay open at this time of night.'

'Ah! In the day they serve men from the docks but at night a lot of young people from the town go there, almost like a club. It is cheap and they have a juke box and if he is in a good mood Joe will let you push the tables back and dance. Sometimes I go there, it is very good.'

A few minutes later Wycliffe was down in the street again. It was properly dark now; if you turned away from the glare of the docks you could see the stars against a velvet sky. He crossed the road to the café, looked up and saw Kathy at her window once more, waved and went inside.

A warm chippy smell. A counter with a coffee machine, a tea urn and a cash register, a few bar stools and behind the counter a fat man with a bald head reading the evening paper. But from the other side of a glass partition, plenty of noise, a juke box in full cry. Behind the counter an open door led into a kitchen.

'Evening.' The fat man stirred himself reluctantly.

Wycliffe produced his warrant card. The fat man, who must be Joe, looked at it indifferently. 'I suppose it's about that business across the way?' He nodded in the direction of the Marina. 'Your chaps have been in here already.'

'I know. You told them the girl came in here for her meals and that she came alone.'

'That's right. She did.' Joe looked at the superintendent through innocent china-blue eyes. 'Since they was here I been thinking and the more I think the more convinced I am – I seen that girl before.'

'Here?'

'Where else? I never go anywhere.'

A waitress came through from the other side of the partition, filled two cups at the coffee machine, rang up one and four and withdrew.

'You have a lot of young people in and out of here in the course of an evening, do you know them all?'

He shook his head. 'No, not all but I don't encourage strangers unless they got somebody I know with 'em. It's easier to keep the peace that way. You know where you stand.' He smoothed a massive hand over his bald head. 'How old would you say she was?'

'Twenty-one, give or take a few months.'

'That means she could have been coming in here anything up to say five or even six years ago.' He shook his head. 'I shall have to think about it.'

The street door opened and a girl put her head round, 'Joyce here tonight, Joe?'

'Ain't seen her.'

The head hesitated then made up its mind. 'OK. Thanks. See you!'

'Are you married?'

The fat man looked surprised. 'Me?' He laughed. 'I'm married all right with three kids and they're married too.'

He looked at Wycliffe speculatively. 'Like a coffee?'

Wycliffe nodded and waited while Joe drew two cups. When they were steaming on the counter he produced half a bottle of rum and added a tot to each. 'I've never known a copper yet who didn't prefer it this way.'

Two youths came through from the inner room. 'Night, Joe!'

'You're off early tonight, what's up?'

'We're going fishing with Freddie Bates, there's mackerel out in the bay – millions of 'em.'

Wycliffe and the fat man sipped their coffee. In the mellow mood of the moment he would have given a great deal to go fishing all night in the bay with Freddie Bates, or he would have swopped jobs with the fat man if that had been possible. Of course, what you see of another man's life is just the tip of the iceberg. He brought out his pouch and offered it across the counter but Joe refused. 'Don't smoke.'

'You must know a good many of the docks people?'

'I've been on their doorstep for thirty years.'

Wycliffe put a match to his pipe. 'If somebody wanted to get a man out of the country through this port – no questions asked – could it be done?'

The china-blue eyes studied him with disquieting serenity. 'I suppose it could; there'd be a risk of course.'

'How would you set about it?'

Joe smiled showing two rows of ostentatiously false teeth. 'I wouldn't, I like my peace of mind too much. But I suppose it could be done in one of two ways. A suitable man might get hold of false credentials and sign on as crew . . . '

'A suitable man, you say – that means he'd have to be a seaman?'

'He'd need to know his way round a ship.'

'And if he didn't?'

'Then he'd have to stow away and if he was going to do that and get ashore in a foreign port he'd need at least one friend in the crew, preferably somebody with a bit of authority.'

'You think it could be done?'

Joe smoothed his bald head. 'Of course it can be done. It would probably be more difficult with the bigger ships but one of the smallish foreigners . . . You might not have to search too long before you found even a skipper with a blind eye provided there was a big enough bait.'

'A thousand pounds?'

A shake of the head. 'I'm not up with the prices but in my opinion you'd get all you want for that.'

'Thanks.'

Joe grinned. 'Thinking of emigrating?'

'Something like that.'

Wycliffe moved away from the counter and pushed open the glass panelled door which led to the café. A long room with tables down both sides, green painted walls with advertisements for cigarettes and soft drinks, a couple of bagatelle machines and the juke box. Most of the tables were occupied by long haired youngsters of indeterminate sex. No dancing tonight, presumably because Joe's mood was inauspicious. He walked up the aisle between the tables glanced at indifferently. You would need to be a Siamese dwarf with three legs to really engage their attention. The waitress was at the end tables. Her skirt was so short that every time she bent over a table she showed her behind, but she seemed amiable. 'The girl that was killed? Yes, she used to come here. Are you a reporter?'

'Police.'

'Oh!' Her disappointment was obvious.

'Where did she sit?'

'This one by the window.'

'She arrived in the town on Sunday evening and she died on Tuesday night. How many meals did she have here? Lunch and evening meal on Monday, lunch and evening meal on Tuesday – four meals – is that it?'

'She came here Sunday night.'

'All right – five. Five meals but she sticks in your mind as though she'd been a regular customer for months . . . '

The girl swished crumbs from the plastic top of an empty table and wiped the surface with a damp cloth. 'Well, she would. I mean at lunch time she'd be the only woman in the place except me and Nelly and in the evening, well, she wasn't one of this lot, was she?'

'Too old?'

The little carmine lips screwed up. 'Not so much that but she was different.'

'How?'

'I dunno. The way she was dressed for one thing. She had style, and, for another, there was something about her, she was so small and yet she was . . . well, I know it sounds funny but she was perfect. I mean you could look at her as much as you like and you couldn't find anything wrong with her . . . '

'Did she spend long over her meals?'

'Quite a while. She brought a book and read, and after she had finished eating she would sit there with a cup of coffee, reading. She wasn't in any hurry to go.'

'She had lunch here twice when the place must have been full of men, did any of them get fresh with her?'

She shook her head. 'No, they watched her but they never spoke a word to her, not even a whistle.'

'So that each time she came in she sat at that table alone and spoke to no-one but you – is that right?'

'Well yes, except for one lunch time, it must have been Tuesday, a man came in and sat at her table.'

'A stranger?'

'No, a local, a man called Pellow – Dippy Pellow; he comes in for a meal now and then. He runs one of the launches that tend on the boats.'

'What sort of chap is he to look at?'

She screwed up her face. 'A dark little man, he must be forty-five to fifty. If you ask me a nasty bit of work.'

'In what way?'

She shrugged. 'For one thing he can't keep his hands to himself. I mean, at his age – it's disgusting!'

'Did you get the impression that he came here to meet her or was it by chance?'

She hesitated. 'I never thought, but now you mention it, perhaps he did. Don't you whistle at me, I aren't your dog! Some people!' The rebuke was for a youth, trying to attract her attention by whistling.

'Did the girl do more than pass the time of day with him?'

'Oh yes, they seemed quite matey. I was surprised.'

'You didn't hear anything of what they said to each other?'

She frowned. 'Believe me, mister, I got something better to do here at lunch time than listen to the customers. Which reminds me,' she added curtly, 'I got work to do now.'

'Wait!' His sudden peremptory manner brought her up short. 'Did she have anything to say to you?'

'Nothing more than just to give her order and say the usual things – nice weather an' all that.'

'You've lived in the town a long time?'

'All my life.'

'You didn't recognize or feel that she was familiar?'

The waitress looked puzzled. 'No, should I have?'

Wycliffe shook his head. 'I've no idea!'

He walked back to his hotel. A moist breeze had sprung up from the west and the air was chilly. Rain tomorrow. He pulled up the collar of his jacket and wished that he had worn his raincoat. The street was almost deserted and he felt depressed. An evening newspaper placard fluttered in the breeze: *Police Baffled by Hotel Murder*. For once they were dead right. Thirty-six hours after the discovery of the girl's body he ought to know a great deal more about her. Was she working for the Masson-Smythes? And if so, doing what? According to them they had kicked her out but according to Sadie she had left of her own free will knowing enough to put them both in gaol. Had she tried her hand at blackmail? That would account for the money and in certain circles blackmail is as good a way to get yourself murdered as any other. But surely not in the way this girl had been killed? Unless Masson-Smythe . . . But would he pay her hush money, make love to her, kill her and go away leaving the money? It didn't make sense. And why at a fifth-rate dump like the Marina? And where did the fugitive Allen come in?

At the back of his mind he had an idea which made sense of a good deal. He had scarcely realized that it was there until he had spoken to the café owner about stowaways. Now, to cheer himself up, he elaborated it in unaccustomed detail.

Assume that the girl had left the Voodoo as she said to go to a job in London. There she takes up with Allen, a small-time crook with ambitions beyond his class. He is nicked and charged, among other things, with attempted murder but he gets away. What if the Masson-Smythes were Travel Agents? Travel Agents for the underworld? Such organizations exist. From time to time the police uncover one and clean it up but where there is a demand . . . This might not be a bad base, especially with agents in some of the other ports of the south and west. If the girl had ferreted out their secret while she worked at the Voodoo the knowledge would seem heaven sent with her boy friend on the run. Allen is sent to lie low at the Marina until the girl arrives with the money. There she is contacted by Dippy Pellow who runs a launch . . . But why does it fall through? Why is she killed? Above all, why is she disfigured?

Wycliffe sighed audibly and drew curious glances from a couple in a shop doorway. He had to admit that there was only one aspect of the case which interested him – the fact that a girl of twenty-one had been strangled. Crimes of violence appalled him and murder most of all. There can be no restitution. Wycliffe numbered among the people he would call friends thieves, pick-pockets, pimps and forgers, but never once had he felt the least glimmer of sympathy or understanding for the man who used violence as one of the tools of his trade.

It was half past eleven when he reached the hotel and still there were two or three dedicated drinkers on the bar stools, the barman yawning behind his hand. Wycliffe ordered a brandy and drank it off.

'Good night to you.'

'Good night, superintendent.'

Now that they knew who he was there would be no chance of maintaining the illusion of being on holiday.

He went upstairs to bed and at last slipped in beside his wife. She spoke drowsily: 'Anything happened?'

'Enough.' He kissed her good night, turned over and fell asleep at once.

CHAPTER SIX

Drizzling rain from a slate grey sky. Friday morning. Wycliffe sat at a table in the HQ room looking at a photograph. Gill was having his first smoke of the day, perched on the edge of the same table, like a gargoyle. A detective constable hammered away at his report, his papers among the empty teacups. Wycliffe was absorbed: the photograph showed a girl with shoulder length hair gleaming in the light, fine open features, the forehead broad; thin, gently arched eyebrows, eyes wide, with long curving lashes, delicate nostrils and exquisite lips slightly parted and glistening with moisture as though she had just drawn her tongue across them. Yet this was the picture of a dead girl, the product of the pathologist's knowledge of anatomy and the police photographer's skill. Wycliffe had only to supply colour from memory and imagination, the hair was auburn, the eyes blue – almost violet, the skin . . .

'It's a work of bloody art!' Jim Gill said. 'It could have been on the front page of every newspaper tomorrow morning, now it's wasted.'

Wycliffe put the photograph down. 'She hasn't been officially identified yet so let them go ahead and publish. It will be interesting to see who admits to knowing her – and who doesn't.'

He stood up. 'I'm going to see Collins.'

The rain was hardly enough to keep people indoors but enough to make them wonder why they came out. The clock over the post office showed nine thirty-five and already visitors were trailing through the streets wondering whether to risk a boat trip or, if they didn't, what to do with the day. The narrow street was completely blocked by lorries unloading and several shopkeepers were still washing down their fronts.

At the bookshop a little man with brown eyes like buttons was cleaning the windows and had to move his ladder for Wycliffe to enter. Inside two girls were dusting down the shelves with feather dusters and one of them came over to him.

'I want to see Mr Collins.'

The girl obviously wanted to ask him his business but the blank impassive stare which he had cultivated as part of his stock-in-trade discouraged her and she went off down the shop, wiggling her bottom to show that she was not really impressed. He thought that she had gone to fetch Collins but he was mistaken. After a minute or two she came back with an older woman, a woman in her middle thirties, prickly with efficiency, the sort who has convinced herself that a business career is superior to a man in bed. 'Can I help you?'

'I want to see Mr Collins.'

Pursed lips. 'I'm Miss Rogers, I look after most of the firm's affairs.'

Defeated after all. 'This is personal. I am Detective Chief Superintendent Wycliffe.'

He saw her quick frown and, though her manner remained distant and slightly aggressive, he felt that she had become uneasy.

At the rear of the shop, hidden by bookcases, was a white painted iron spiral staircase, and a sign, pointing up it: *Secondhand Department*. He followed her up the steps and into the distilled mustiness of thousands of old books, a bitter sweet smell even to the booklover. The room was of indeterminate size, crammed with bookcases except for a clearing at the top of the stairs where there were two desks set near a window which overlooked the harbour. At the one nearest him an old lady sat knitting. She had an old fashioned box-till, an account book and a notice which read: *All purchases to be paid for here*. The other desk was littered with papers but there was no-one sitting at it.

'Where's Mr Willie?'

The old lady stopped knitting and looked at Wycliffe. She had cultivated her age; silver hair meticulously cared for; pouting, rather bad-tempered lips, lightly rouged; soft skinned fleshy cheeks with a dusting of powder to hide an unhealthy flush. 'Who is this?'

'A gentleman to see Mr Willie – where is he? Is he up in the flat?'

A measured silence through which the old lady asserted her refusal to be questioned. 'I'm Mrs Collins, you wish to see my son? What about?' She turned to the younger woman. 'No need for you to wait, Miss Rogers.'

It was an absurd situation though the tension was obvious. Miss Rogers stood irresolute for a moment, thought better of making a scene, and clattered off down the iron stairs making them vibrate. The old lady watched her go then turned to Wycliffe. 'You were saying?' But Wycliffe was saved the trouble of having to repeat himself.

'You wish to see me?' Willie Collins himself. Excessively tall, a scholarly stoop, pebble glasses distorting his eyes. He looked forty or more but a second look decided that he might be younger; his close-cropped sandy hair was almost boyish though his clothes drooped from his shoulders as though from the wasted frame of an old man.

'Detective Chief Superintendent Wycliffe, Mr Collins.'

Willie blinked down at him. 'Perhaps we should go somewhere where we can talk.' He darted bird-like glances from his mother to the superintendent and back again, the light glinting on his spectacles.

'Willie . . . '

'Yes, mother?'

The old lady hesitated. 'All right, take the superintendent up to the flat, I'll be there directly.'

'There's no need, mother.'

'Of course I shall come up!'

A small gesture of resignation. 'This way, superintendent.'

Through the bookcase maze to a green baize door and out on to a carpeted landing. Stairs down to a tiny hall and up to the flat.

'We have a side entrance, you see.'

Their sitting room overlooked the narrow chasm of the street and it was not a pleasant room. Wycliffe was vaguely aware of a sense of oppression, not entirely due to the poor light, the massive old-fashioned furniture, the sombre browns and fawns. But more to a feeling that this was a room in which people never lived. He would have sworn that the piano in its walnut case was never played, there was no wireless, no television, no books, newspapers, magazines – no knitting even. Yet within seconds the door opened and a woman bustled in. 'Oh! I didn't know there was anybody here.' Obvious that she was lying.

Willie was put out. 'This gentleman wants to talk to me, Aunt Jane.' But her fixed bland smile forced him to introductions. 'Miss Collins – my father's sister . . . '

She was at least twenty years younger than Willie's mother; leaner, harder, with a hint of fanaticism in her protuberant eyes and thin hard lips. Perhaps she had been born to be a nun and missed a turning somewhere, but she would certainly have looked at home in a convent of one of the stricter orders. She had mannish features accentuated by an Eton-crop hairstyle, a bi-tonal voice like an adolescent boy's, and her frame was innocent of curves. 'My dear Willie! What have you been doing to bring a Chief Superintendent visiting us? I'm sure that it must be something quite dreadful!' Her boisterously arch manner irritated. She made no move to go and after an awkward silence she seated herself on a straight-backed chair and waited.

Wycliffe was by the window, peering out between the narrow gap in the curtains; he could look into a room across the street where two girls sat at a table piled high with flowers. They were putting them into bunches. Another world.

'When did you last hear from your wife, Mr Collins?'

Willie was still standing, fiddling with a china ornament on the mantelpiece.

'My nephew's wife left him two years ago and he hasn't heard from her since. It distresses him to speak of her, superintendent.' The melting glance she threw at Willie was not lost on the superintendent.

He produced the reconstructed photograph. 'Is this your wife, Mr Collins?'

Willie took the photograph and stared at it myopically. 'Where did you get this?'

'Is it your wife?'

'Yes.'

'Let me see it, dear.' Aunt Jane took the photograph from him, glanced at it and handed it to Wycliffe. What she had seen seemed to reassure her for she became more relaxed. 'It's her all right.'

'What is it, Willie?' His mother, flushed and out of breath. 'So you're here, Jane!' She looked from her sister-in-law to her son. 'Do you really want your aunt to hear all your business, Willie?'

Willie shrugged.

Wycliffe got down to business in self defence. 'I expect that you have heard of the death of a young woman at the Marina Hotel?'

Willie must have guessed what was coming but he gave no sign.

'I'm sorry to tell you that it was your wife who was killed – murdered.'

'Murdered.' Willie repeated the word in a curiously flat tone which seemed to signify complete acceptance.

'She was strangled.'

An incredibly smug look on the old lady's face. 'Well, it's nothing to do with us, superintendent! That girl walked out of here two years ago.'

Wycliffe said nothing. Willie might not have heard for all the impression the news seemed to have made on him. The old lady went on, her voice complacent like the cooing of a well-fed pigeon. 'Something was bound to happen to a girl like that – she was *wicked*! If she's been punished it's no more than she deserves.'

Aunt Jane remained unmoved but she frowned at her sister-in-law. 'That's foolish talk, Ada, it's natural that the superintendent will want to ask us questions.'

Wycliffe produced the ring which had been taken from the dead girl's finger. 'Was this her wedding ring?'

Willie reached out to take it but his mother forestalled him. She turned to Wycliffe, 'This ring belonged to my mother, she was called Jessica and she married William. You can see the two initials inside. Willie gets his name from both sides of the family . . . ' She fingered the ring for a moment and her face softened in recollection, but then the customary pout returned. 'That girl had no business to take it!'

'Don't be silly, Ada! You gave it her, it was her wedding ring!' Aunt Jane snapped. 'In any case you've changed your tune, when she first came here nothing was too good for her. I saw what she was from the start but you'd take no notice of me!'

Wycliffe never ceased to marvel at the scarcity value of human compassion and the meagre currency of charity. 'You are required to identify your wife's body, Mr Collins, and after that you will be asked to make a statement.' These people sickened him.

The old lady bristled. 'I really don't see why my son should be involved in the scandal surrounding this woman. He is respected in the town . . . '

'For God's sake shut up, mother!' Willie bleated and the outburst was so obviously unprecedented that it was followed by stunned silence.

His mother recovered first. 'How dare you speak to your mother like that!'

Wycliffe happened to be looking at Aunt Jane and saw the satisfaction on her face. He was physically as well as mentally ill at ease, the room was close, airless, and he could feel the perspiration round his neck soaking into his collar. Willie looked at him, a pleading look. 'Let's get out of here!' Willie got up and he followed him out of the room and across the passage. 'This is my room, I work and sleep here . . . '

The room looked out on the harbour, it was large, oblong, and more of a study than a bedroom. A narrow bunk tucked against one wall was the only apparent concession to sleeping. Apart from this the two long walls were occupied by benches with drawers below and shelves above. Several of the shelves were crowded with rank upon rank of brightly coloured toy soldiers, drawn up in parade ground order. The walls between the shelves were entirely hidden by coloured prints of eighteenth and nineteenth century uniforms. Under the benches, the smaller drawers were labelled: *Colours; Artillery; Small Arms* . . . the large ones, with the names of battles: *Ramillies; Waterloo; Sedan* . . . The wall by the door was a single nest of bookshelves reaching from floor to ceiling and all the books seemed to be concerned with warfare and the strategy of war, lives of famous generals and technical works on weapons.

Wycliffe looked round with appreciation. This was the sort of room of which he approved – professionally. It told him something of its owner, in this case, probably enough to prise off the lid of Willie's reserve. But he would have to go warily. He picked up a splendid hussar from the array of cavalry and examined it, expressing his admiration. 'I suppose these are accurate?'

'Of course! There would be no point in having them otherwise. I don't play with toy soldiers!' A practised answer to the soft impeachment.

'You are a student of warfare?'

The eyes behind the thick lenses were cautious. 'Of the eighteenth and nineteenth centuries. I know little of earlier times and less of modern war, the very thought of which appalls me.'

Wycliffe nodded, replacing the horseman carefully in his rank. Collins pointed to a comfortable looking wing-backed chair. 'Sit down, smoke if you want to.' He spoke in nervous jerks. 'I don't smoke myself.' He seated himself in a swivel chair by his desk and seemed to gain confidence in doing so. 'You wanted to ask me some questions about Julie?'

Wycliffe filled and lit his pipe. Collins seemed to be taking the news of his wife's death remarkably calmly – if it was news. But you could never tell with his sort; often, in self defence, they seemed able to contrive barriers of the mind, compartments in which unpleasant events could be more or less isolated, held for a time in cold storage. 'You don't strike me as a violent man, Mr Collins.'

Collins's quick glance darted round the room. 'Violent?' He made a broad gesture. 'You mean all this? No, I'm not in the least violent, quite the contrary. That's probably why my interest in war is historical. The present and the recent past are too immediate for me, but the battles of Marlborough and Napoleon are sufficiently remote for me to be objective about them. I can look at the strategy of a war or the tactics of a battle in much the same way as I might consider the problems presented by a game of chess.' He was undoubtedly shy, reticent, but he could not resist the chance to explain himself, probably because such opportunities came seldom. He fiddled with his blotter and scribbling pad, placing them geometrically on his desk, then he added, 'I *abhor* violence!'

'You think that it is never justified?'

A period of hesitation. 'I do think that but I also think that it is inevitable, human nature being what it is.'

Wycliffe dimly apprehended that as long as his questions remained general the scholar in Willie would see that he got honest answers. But he was less certain what would happen when the questions became personal. At heart, he believed, Willie was still the gangling gawky youth who had been the butt of his schoolfellows, the one who skulked in a corner of the playground, dreading to be noticed.

But Willie was still worrying away at the problem posed by Wycliffe's last question. 'I think that for any man, however mild, there is a point beyond which he may resort to violence.' He smiled vaguely. 'Call it the threshold of violence. We each have our different thresholds and those for whom it is low soon acquire a reputation for habitual violence while others have to be faced with extreme provocation before . . . ' His voice trailed off.

'But even the worm will turn at last – is that what you are saying?'

Collins looked at him, hesitated for a moment, then nodded. 'Yes.'

'How old are you, Mr Collins?'

'I am thirty-eight.'

'And your wife?'

'She is – was, twenty, almost twenty-one.' He crossed his spindly legs and started to beat a tattoo on his knee with his fingers. 'I married Julie two-and-a-half years ago when she was eighteen.' He spoke the name Julie in a special way; it occurred to Wycliffe that it was in a similar manner that priests spoke the name of Christ.

'Her parents?'

'She was an orphan, both her parents were killed in an air crash while she was still a child and she was in the care of the local authority – boarded out, I think that is the expression.'

'She was unhappy?'

'On the contrary, I think that she was quite at home with her foster parents. She had been with them for nine or ten years and they regarded her as their daughter. I think that they would have adopted her but for some legal quibble.'

'They raised no objection to her marrying a man seventeen years older?'

'No. Julie had to apply to the Court but her application was supported by her foster parents and by the local authority.'

'Was she pregnant?'

The restless fingers stopped tapping. 'She was not!'

Wycliffe hardly knew what to ask. He wanted some flesh to clothe the bare bones of this unlikely romance. A young, attractive girl immures herself with two shrewish women in order to marry a shy studious man twice her age. There must have been something.

'How did you first meet her?'

It was obvious that the question revived memories which had become painful. He spoke in a low voice and with long pauses. 'She was at school studying for her "A" levels. She was very serious about her work and her foster parents encouraged her. She read widely and she came to the shop first to buy cheap second-hand books – cheap copies of the poets. Then she found that I was interested in literature and she began to discuss her work with me. She would come in after school or on a Saturday and spend a lot of time in the bookroom. I would join her when I could and we would talk about what she had read, about her lessons, and we would plan her future work.'

'At that time you never met her outside?'

'I told you . . . '

'Always in the bookroom with your mother sitting at the cash desk?'

'Why yes. Mother is always there when the shop is open; she doesn't have to be there but it was her job when father was in the business and it would hurt her if she thought she was no longer needed.'

'Rather onerous conditions for courtship, surely?'

Willie flushed. 'There was no question of courtship!'

'But you married the girl!' He felt that he was moving in a realm outside the usual flesh and blood one that he knew, a world, perhaps, where an apt quotation took the place of hot hands in the back of the stalls. Not one that Julie would be at home in, of that he felt certain. 'Whose idea was it? Yours or hers?'

Willie took off his glasses and began to polish them for they had misted over. 'Actually it was my mother's.'

His mother's! Unexpected but it made sense. 'Your mother had a good opinion of Julie, then?'

'Yes, mother thought her a pleasant, well brought up girl.'

And mother thought too, 'A young girl can be guided – *moulded*.' With Willie well on the wrong side of thirty the alternative might be some mature woman with a mind of her own. Wycliffe thought that he could set the scene and write the script:

'It's time you thought seriously about getting married, Willie.'

'I'm in no hurry. In any case, the chance would be a fine thing!' Forced joke.

'Don't be absurd, Willie! Scores of girls would jump at the chance.'

'All I can say is, I never come across them.'

'One in particular.'

'Oh?'

'Julie.'

'Julie! Don't be absurd, mother! She's only a child.'

'She's a woman, Willie. She knows it if you don't!'

'In any case it's ridiculous, Julie never thinks of me like that. To her I'm just an old buffer who helps her a bit with her work – just like another teacher.'

'In Julie's eyes you can do no wrong – I know.'

'Nonsense!'

'Ask her.'

And in the end, of course, he did, as he did most things his mother wished. And because he was already in love with her youth and her mind, because he had a romantic vision of a relationship which was intellectual but deeply affectionate, because her foster parents saw it as a good match and because Julie wanted to get out of her council house home – they married.

That was it, or something like it.

The room was quiet, Wycliffe smoked peacefully, Willie stared at the carpet.

'Can men more injure women than to say
They love them for that, by which they are not they?'

The sentiment might well have appealed to Willie, but not, Wycliffe felt sure, to Julie, not to the girl he had seen lying dead at the Marina.

'What happened?'

Outside the pleasure boats were setting out across the harbour, some bound for the creeks and wooded reaches of the river, others for the more adventurous trip across the bay. A watery gleam of sunshine gave them encouragement. The siren of the ferry boat blasted, sharp, angry, as she changed course to avoid running down a dinghy drifting across her path with sails flapping. Wycliffe could see it all, just sitting there. In such a room he would never do any work.

'What went wrong?'

A stupid question about a situation which had never been right but Collins would not see it like that.

'I don't know. At first everything seemed to go well, then Julie started going out in the evenings, she would stay out late and offer no explanation. In the end she just went off.'

It seemed impossible to make any contact, to find common ground. 'Was she a virgin?'

Willie coloured. 'No.' His eyes darted round the room like an animal trying to escape. 'She told me that she had been . . . that she had been raped by a boy when she was fourteen.'

'Did you believe her?'

It was cruelty. 'I don't know.'

'The sexual side of your marriage – was it satisfactory?'

Willie could not have suffered more on the rack. 'I don't know. Why do you ask me these questions?'

'When she left you, where did she go?'

The relief was painful to see. 'She got a job in the town – in cabaret. Mother could never forgive her for that, she thought she did it on purpose to humiliate us.'

'And you – could you forgive her?'

The glasses glinted in the light. 'I had nothing to forgive, it was I who was wrong. I realize now that there was no life in this place for a young girl. I should have known, but if she had told me I would have given her anything . . . ' There was pathos in his simplicity.

But it wasn't difficult to imagine the situation. Julie treading on eggshells until she began to feel secure. Timid at first, overawed, watched by the two women. 'We don't do it that way dear! Never mind – you'll learn. We all have to be patient, don't we?' And a husband who believed that love could be equated with romance.

Was that how it had been? Or was there something more sinister behind it all?

'What did you do in the evenings before Julie started to go out?'

He looked surprised by the question. 'In the evenings? Julie used to play three-handed bridge with mother and my aunt.'

'And you?'

'I worked in here.'

'Did you expect her to leave you?'

'No, it came as a great shock.' He matched the tips of his fingers together and studied the result. 'She left a letter for mother which upset her very much.'

'Did you try to get her back?'

He nodded. It seemed for a moment that he could not trust himself to speak. 'Then she went away altogether.'

'And you didn't see her again until . . . until when, Mr Collins?'

'I never saw her again.'

'When she left, did she take any money with her?'

'She may have had a few pounds – not much.'

'She did not steal money from you or from the business?'

'Certainly not!' Collins looked startled. 'Why do you ask?'

Why did he ask? Wycliffe looked at the lean anxious face, at the tense body. Not a modicum of repose. What did he expect the poor devil to say in answer to all his questions? I killed my wife? Was that the object of the exercise? That, or to prove that he had done no such thing. Either way it was preposterous. If this man had murdered his wife it was because at thirty-eight he was still adolescent, because all his self control, all the restraints that were normal to him had been eroded by consuming jealousy; it was because he had a silly, selfish mother; because he had been a fool to marry a precocious child. Because of anything except wanting her dead. Now he had to live with his remorse – if he was guilty. What good would questions do him or Julie or anyone? And if there was no guilt then Wycliffe's very presence in the house was an impertinence.

The mood came and went. Julie was dead by violence and violence must be contained. When he had doubts about his calling, and he had them often, that was his answer.

'Who were her foster parents? I shall have to see them.'

'They are called Little. He is a welder at the docks and they live on the Three Fields Estate – 3, Trevellas Way.'

Wycliffe made a note. There was much more he wanted to know but he believed in short interviews with return visits. He stood up. 'Well, Mr Collins, if you are ready, we will get it over.'

'Now?' A scared look behind the thick lenses.
'These things won't wait.'
'All right. I'd better tell them. How long will it take?'
'You should be back in two hours.'
Wycliffe waited while Willie talked to his mother and aunt. Then they had to walk to the police station where Wycliffe had left his car. As they made their way through the busy streets a surprising number of people greeted Willie in a friendly fashion but he hardly seemed to see them.
'You are very popular in the town.'
'I've lived here all my life.'
They had to drive ten miles to the County Hospital and Willie sat staring at the road ahead. Wycliffe tried to start a conversation several times without result. It was only as they were pulling into the hospital car park that he started a topic of his own.
'Was there anything found in her room?'
'What sort of thing?'
He was quick to disclaim any preconceived idea. 'I don't know – anything.'
'A thousand pounds in used notes.'
Willie said nothing.
Dr Franks was in the pathology building and Wycliffe went to see him first. 'I've brought the husband.'
'Husband?' Franks's brows went up. 'I hadn't thought of her with a husband, is she local?'
'More or less. I wanted to ask you, did she dope?'
'Dope? No. There's no evidence of habitual drug taking – why?'
Wycliffe shrugged. 'Don't bother with it.'
As they went in, Franks whispered, 'You've warned him?'
'No.'

The white light shone down on Julie's shrouded form. 'Just one good look, Mr Collins, and I must warn you that what you will see will distress you.' He nodded to the attendant who lifted the sheet. 'Is that your wife, Mr Collins?'

Willie looked down at the body, he stared as though mesmerized; then he gave a queer pathetic little cry and collapsed on the tiles.

CHAPTER SEVEN

'Shall we eat out tonight?'

'If you like. Anywhere in mind?'

'A club, a place called the Voodoo, food, drinks, dancing and a floorshow.'

She looked at him suspiciously. 'It hardly sounds your sort of place.'

'It isn't but I think it might be interesting.'

Since the previous evening the club had been under observation. They had been lucky, an ex-policeman kept a tobacconist's shop across the road from the club and it was a simple matter to put a man in the stockroom over the shop. He had a personal radio and there was a telephone in the next room. His brief was vague, to note all the comings and goings when the club was closed and to try to spot any *known* persons entering or leaving when it was open. The watcher had Allen's photograph and instructions to look out for him in particular.

'He wouldn't be fool enough to try to hide out there,' Gill said but Wycliffe was less certain.

Keeping 'obo' sounds simple enough until you have tried spotting someone from a photograph, simple enough if you have the sort of memory which is an index of faces. Really simple only if you have a sixth sense for the job. Wycliffe had kept obo on countless occasions; having a room for it was luxury. For him, sitting in the soft darkness, looking out on the life of the street would have been a pleasure rather than a chore. A flask of coffee and a packet of sandwiches . . . But it is not a permissible recreation for chief superintendents. All the same he refused to be left out entirely. He decided that he wanted to put Masson-Smythe on edge without making any overt move against him. So he found himself an excuse for dining there.

Membership was by no means exclusive, a pound paid at the desk and a signature in the register, but the food and drink were expensive and there was a minimum charge.

Helen looked round the room with interest. It was dimly but cleverly lit by a red glow from hidden lamps so that the totem figures, the voodoo masks and the murals achieved their maximum effect. When they arrived several couples were dancing but most were at the tables eating. They were shown to a table not far from the stage and presented with monstrous menus which were difficult to read in the dim light.

'Why are these places always so dark?' Helen grumbled.

'I think it's supposed to make you feel naughty.'

'It makes me wonder if the cutlery is clean.'

They ordered roast lamb masquerading as *Filet d'agneau au four* and a bottle of Beaujolais.

During the meal Wycliffe saw Thelma from time to time. She moved among the tables saying the right things to the right people but she did not reach the tables near the stage. Her blue gown, high waisted in the classical style, made the best of her Junoesque figure. 'A striking woman,' Helen said.

'I prefer something more cuddly,' Wycliffe said. 'With her I should always be afraid of being eaten afterwards. Shall we have liqueurs?'

They were about to order when Wycliffe spotted Masson-Smythe himself, immaculate in evening dress, brooding over the floor. He saw them and came over, suave, ingratiating. Wycliffe introduced him to Helen.

'You are having liqueurs? Curaçao? Allow me. I insist!'

He instructed the waiter. 'I have a rather special Triple Sec which I keep for my friends . . . May I?' He seated himself at their table.

Wycliffe was astonished at the change in him but felt that this solicitous restaurateur act was a bit overdone.

Helen congratulated him on his club. 'Surprising to find such a place in a small town.'

'It doesn't make a fortune.' Masson-Smythe laughed. 'In fact, during the off-season we do no more than break even but we have to stay open to keep the nucleus of a competent staff.' He looked round with a certain pride at the well filled room. 'As you see at this time of year we do pretty well.'

'Have you always been in this business, Mr Masson-Smythe?'

He beckoned to the cigarette girl and selected two cigars from her tray. 'Mr Wycliffe?'

'That's very civil of you,' Wycliffe said, accepting a cigar.

When they were smoking he turned once more to Helen. 'No, I haven't always been in this business. I was chief steward on one of the Atlantic liners for a number of years. When I got tired of shuttling to and fro and had made enough money, I went to work for a London club to learn the business, then I started here.' Was there a challenge in the look he gave the superintendent? From time to time he dabbed with a white silk handkerchief at the beads of perspiration on his upper lip and once he removed and polished his glasses, squinting painfully while he did so.

Soon Helen was telling him about the twins. 'Have you a family, Mr Smythe?'

'Unfortunately, no. This business and a family don't mix I'm afraid.'

'You don't find it necessary to employ a bouncer?' Wycliffe showing a professional interest.

Masson-Smythe grinned. 'We get very little trouble and if the need arises I can give quite a good account of myself.' His candour was disarming.

They chatted amicably until the cabaret was due to start then he left them.

'What did you make of him?'

Helen was thoughtful. 'Smooth. Did you notice his face? He's had some sort of operation and plastic surgery to disguise the scar.'

Of course! That explained the facial immobility – his lack of expression.

'I also noticed that Thelma hardly took her eyes off us the whole time he was here.'

The bandleader announced the first act of the cabaret in a throaty contralto which made the audience laugh, putting them in the mood. A comedian told a seemingly endless stream of blue jokes and he was followed by a female impersonator whose sex might have been questioned anyway. A pretty girl with a guitar sang folk songs and the audience joined in the choruses. Picked out by a pink spotlight in the darkened room she looked young and appealing in her white mini-dress and everyone felt sentimental. Then it was Sadie's turn. It took her seven minutes of more or less graceful pirouettes and postures before she finally parted with her G-string and made her tour of the tables, her modesty protected by two Japanese fans. What her act lacked in skill was made up by her obvious desire to please and in this, to judge from the applause, she succeeded. When she saw the superintendent, she blushed.

Wycliffe looked at his watch. 'Eleven fifteen.'

'They don't close until three and there's another show with different acts in an hour . . . ' Helen was enjoying herself.

Wycliffe stood up. 'I'll be back.' He made his way across

the floor now crowded with dancers, out into the foyer. One or two couples were sitting out on the banquettes and a noisy crowd of Midlanders, just arrived, were being persuaded to sign the book. He pushed open the door marked *Adams* into the elegant washroom, all white tiles and gleaming chrome. He presented himself to the wall thinking vaguely about the case but he had had enough to drink to feel gratifyingly detached and benevolent. A cistern flushed in one of the cubicles behind him and he heard the sound of a door catch. A vague reflection of movement in the shining tiles and then a violent blow to the base of his skull drowned his senses in a great wave of pain.

When he recovered consciousness he was still lying on the tiled floor but now two men were bending over him, one was a stranger but the other was Masson-Smythe. His eyes were magnified by his glasses and Wycliffe was fascinated by them.

'What happened, superintendent? This gentleman found you lying here.'

The question irritated him and the base of his skull ached abominably. 'Somebody slugged me, what do you think happened?' He realized that he was very angry.

'There's a doctor in the club, I've sent for him.'

Wycliffe struggled to his feet. 'I don't need a doctor!' He looked at his watch and his eyes took a moment to focus; it was eleven twenty-five, only ten minutes since he had left Helen. 'Have you told my wife?'

'No . . . Shall I send . . . ?'

'No!'

A third man joined them, the doctor, a dapper little man with white hair but a springy step. Wycliffe was taken, protesting, to the staff rest room and made to sit while the doctor examined him.

'You've got a slight concussion, strictly speaking

you should spend the night in hospital but if you promise . . .'

'I'm going back to my hotel but first I want a telephone . . .' And nothing they could say made any difference. The little doctor took himself off, grumbling, and Masson-Smythe hovered while he shut himself in the plush call-box. He dialled the station.

'Wycliffe here. I strongly suspect that Allen has just left the Voodoo, I want . . .'

'He's been picked up, sir. Wilson, who's on obo opposite the club, saw him come out and radioed in. He was picked up by a Panda . . . Excuse me, sir.' A momentary break. 'They're just bringing him in, sir. Do you want . . . ?'

'I want him locked up!' Wycliffe snapped and slammed down the receiver.

Outside Masson-Smythe had worked himself up into a state of indignation about the outrage committed on his premises but Wycliffe brushed past him growling, 'You need a good bouncer! But if you want to do something you can get me a taxi.'

Back at their table Helen looked at him startled. 'What's wrong?'

'Nothing much. Something's cropped up. Let's go.'

She knew him well enough to keep quiet until they were in the taxi and Masson-Smythe had made his final obsequious apology. 'Now!'

He told her, playing down the incident. 'It's bed for you, my boy!'

His head still ached and he wanted to take a couple of sleeping tablets but Helen was adamant. 'Not on top of all that alcohol!'

Actually he slept soundly until first light. When he woke, his head was still sore, though the pain was more localized. He had a raging thirst which the water from his bedside carafe, flat and warm, did little to cure, and he was tantalized by recollections of the heady chilled beer they serve on the terraces of continental cafés. He tried to occupy his mind with the case. There seemed little doubt that Allen had been hiding out at the Voodoo. If Masson-Smythe was fixing a passage for him it would be the logical place to go when he was forced out of the Marina. It might seem to him to be the last place the police would think of looking for him. Allen could reasonably assume that they would expect him to get as far away from the Marina as possible – not simply to move down the street. But, seeing Wycliffe, his logic deserted him and he panicked.

But what had all this to do with Julie? The only link seemed to be that they were both at the Marina . . . It was no good, he couldn't just lie there with his tongue seeming to swell in his mouth and a taste like sour vinegar. With the greatest care he slid slowly out of bed, but he might have saved himself the trouble.

'What's the matter?'

He mumbled something about the lavatory.

'Are you all right?'

'Fine!'

'You're sure?'

He put on his dressing gown and went out on to the verandah. The harbour lay under a pearly mist which merged into the sky. The land on the other side was a vague insubstantial shape. He could hear the steady chug-chug of a motor launch close by but could not see it, then it emerged abruptly from the mist, glided by and vanished again. An old man wearing a peaked cap and smoking a pipe stood with the tiller caught in his back, immobile as a statue. From somewhere below came the smell of coffee. He stole out of the room and downstairs where his status as a celebrity enabled him to get a cup from the kitchen staff who had just come on duty. He felt better. 'More hangover than concussion,' he told himself and hoped that he was right.

Instead of clearing, by breakfast time the mist had thickened to fog and at intervals they could hear the dismal blare of the fog-signal from the lighthouse in the bay. At nine o'clock, despite protests from Helen, he left for the station on foot. It was not actually raining but water condensed from the supersaturated air as from a steam-bath. He lit his pipe but the tobacco tasted like damp straw.

Saturday morning. The men of the new leisure wondering how to spend the time until *Grandstand*, their women bustling round the house, anxious to get out to do the weekend shopping before the best of everything was sold. Wycliffe felt dull, he had no clear idea what he intended to do. Presumably he would question Allen. The HQ room was empty save for a constable who had been typing and was now collecting his work into neat piles. He was young, probably ambitious.

'What's your name?'

'Rees, sir. Detective Constable.'

'What have you been typing?'

'Sir?'

'I asked you what you've been typing?'

'My report, sir.'

'On what?'

'Enquiries at the railway station, the bus station, taxi ranks and car-hire firms about Allen.'

'Allen is in custody.'

'I know that, sir, but I still have to make my report.'

'Do you think that all this paper work helps you to catch villains?'

The young man was too clever to fall head first into that

one. He considered. 'I think that catching villains is a team job, sir, and the team must know what all its members are doing. In the long run full communication saves work.'

'You've been brainwashed.'

'Sir?'

'You don't believe in the lone-wolf approach?'

'I think that it's out of date and dangerous, sir.'

Catch 'em young! He wondered if he was out of date and dangerous. To be more accurate, he knew that he was out of date and merely wondered whether he had reached the stage of being dangerous. He had no doubt that Deputy Chief Constable Bellings would say that he had. He went into his little room and stood by the window watching the condensed moisture run down the panes. His head still ached. Gill came in and found him there. 'How's the patient?' Wycliffe said nothing and he went on, 'We shall have to box a bit clever on this one. After all, he's already been charged with one major crime and the Yard'll want him back, pronto.'

'They can have him when we've finished with him. I want him as a witness in a murder case and for assaulting a police officer.'

Gill was about to say something but changed his mind. 'I'll be off.'

'Where?'

'To the docks, looking for a bent skipper.'

'Where's Fehling?'

'He's there already, waiting for me. I think he's avoiding you.'

'And well he might!'

When Gill had gone he picked up the telephone. 'Send Allen up . . . and send DC Rees with his notebook.' He hadn't prepared for the interrogation, never given it more than a fleeting thought. After all, he believed in playing things by ear. The great exponent of off-the-cuff detection. Old-fashioned! You get a feeling or you stop being a copper – that's what his first DI used to tell him.

His first reaction on seeing Allen at close quarters was one of incredulity. The man was built like a heavyweight wrestler; yet to hear Kathy talk you would have thought that he was a pitiably weak creature. And to imagine him with the fragile delicacy of the dead girl! The imagination boggled.

His eyes were brown, restless, they shifted focus like the eyes of a nervous animal. Probably his violence sprang from fright. Not that that was any excuse.

Wycliffe looked him up and down coolly. 'I've had you brought here to answer questions concerning the murder of Julie Collins at the Marina Hotel last Tuesday night. I am not concerned with the crime you have been charged with in the Metropolitan Police District – is that clear?'

'I don't know anything about any murder.'

'I said, "Is that clear?" '

'Yes.'

'Sit down.' He nodded to the uniformed constable who removed the cuffs.

Allen sat down and Wycliffe signed to the constable to leave. Rees came in and took his seat in a corner of the room.

'How old are you?'

'You've got it on the sheet.'

'How old are you?'

'Twenty-seven.'

Wycliffe relit his pipe, watching the man over the flickering flame of the match. 'Do you smoke?'

'Cigarettes.'

Wycliffe always carried a packet though he never smoked them; he tossed them over. 'Help yourself.'

Allen's fingers were clumsy and he bruised the cigarette as he drew it from the packet. He stood up, bending over the table for Wycliffe to light it, then he puffed greedily. A moment later he was shaken by a violent spasm of coughing.

'What's the matter with you?'

'I've got a weak chest. I was TB as a kid, perhaps I am again.'

A bid for sympathy? From time to time the bright little brown eyes lighted on Wycliffe only to flit away again as soon as they met his, but they kept coming back. 'He's wondering what to make of me.' Which was all to the good.

'You were staying at the Marina when that girl was killed, why were you there?'

A slow shrug of the massive shoulders. 'It's as good a place as the next to keep out of the way.'

'What was your connection with the girl?'

'None.'

'Your prints were found in the girl's room.'

Allen blew smoke through his nostrils. 'You can't con me, copper!'

'On a photograph in her handbag. How did you get to know her?'

An uneasy movement but no reply.

'She was strangled, then disfigured, her face beaten in with a brass weight which had been used as a door stop. You can imagine.'

The man's hands grasping the arms of his chair tightened and relaxed but he gave no other sign.

'Do I bore you?'

A quick frown.

'Where did you meet her?'

Silence.

Wycliffe reached for the telephone. 'You and I are going for a little trip.' He spoke into the mouthpiece. 'Have my car brought round and tell the constable who delivered Allen to come up.' He was play-acting and he hardly knew with what purpose. 'You too, Rees.'

The constable arrived and Allen was escorted down to Wycliffe's car. He was put into the back seat between his gaolers and Wycliffe drove to the county hospital. The fog was beginning to clear inland, the sun was struggling through and vapour rose from the wet roads and fields. He parked the car and led the way to the pathology building. Allen and his guards were left in a waiting room while he went in search of Dr Franks.

After half an hour Allen was escorted to the mortuary. The central lamp shone down on a covered trolley. Wycliffe and Franks stood on one side while Allen was brought to the other. 'Uncover the face.'

Allen's eyes darted round the room but were drawn at last to the mutilated face of the girl on the trolley. He had prepared himself but even so he could not suppress a movement of revulsion. 'This is your girl friend, Allen, somebody did this to her.'

Allen turned his head away. 'Let me get out of here!'

'Stay where you are!' Wycliffe's voice was like a whiplash. 'What's the matter with you? Don't you recognize her?' He drew the covering sheet further back. 'Perhaps you recognize the mole – look!' Brutal! But the only kind of language Allen and his like would understand.

Allen made a violent movement to shake off the two men who held him but failed. Wycliffe replaced the sheet. 'Have you ever had a blood test?'

It was obvious that the man was near the limit of endurance, but impossible to say which way further pressure would affect him. He might go berserk or simply fold up.

'I want you to have a blood test now; Dr Franks will prick the lobe of your ear and take a drop of blood.'

Allen looked at Wycliffe as a tormented dog looks at its tormentor, dumbly, uncomprehending. Franks came round the trolley, an assistant dabbed Allen's right ear lobe with surgical spirit and Franks produced a tiny lancet and phial. Allen winced as Franks squeezed a few drops of blood into the phial; then another dab of surgical spirit and it was done.

'What's it for?'

Wycliffe glanced at him indifferently. 'Just to check.'

'If you would care to wait in my office . . . ?' As they had planned, Franks led Wycliffe down the corridor to his office. Allen and the two policemen followed. Wycliffe seated himself in the swivel chair behind the metal desk and signed to Allen to take the other chair.

'Wait outside,' to the policemen.

It was a repetition of the scene in Wycliffe's office but now Allen was paler, even more nervous and less sure of himself. 'I didn't kill her.'

Wycliffe regarded him with a detached, impersonal stare. 'We shall see.' He looked round the white aseptic room; even the books and files looked as though they had been sterilized, but the window opened on to a little garden with fuchsias in flower and gladioli flaunting themselves. He had to shift his chair to avoid the direct path of the sunlight.

'Are your parents alive?'

'I don't know.'

'Why were you sent to an approved school in the first place?'

'What does it matter?'

'Was it a sex offence?'

'No!' The denial was prompt and vigorous.

'Women like you, I expect. I mean that you can have all the women you want?'

A glimmer of a smile which vanished at once. 'I've never had to twist their arms.'

'But you despise them?'

He raised his hands in a gesture. 'I take them as they come.'

'I gather that this girl who was murdered was pretty keen on it.'

No answer.

'Do you know what they were doing when he killed her? He was having her. Does that surprise you?'

Allen was sitting bolt upright in his chair, tense, scared.

'Have you ever felt like killing a woman at the very instant when . . . '

'I didn't kill her.'

Wycliffe went on as though he had not spoken. 'Of course, there is another possibility, her room is next to the fire escape, you could have been standing out there watching and then . . . '

The brown eyes were focused steadily on Wycliffe's now and Allen half rose from his chair. What would have happened if Dr Franks had not come bustling in is impossible to say. Ostentatiously Franks handed Wycliffe a slip of paper. 'This is what you are waiting for.' As he went out he gave Allen an inquisitive glance. Wycliffe looked at the paper: *Group A. Rh.+ve.* He folded it and put it carefully into his wallet, then he turned again to Allen. 'I think that you were on the point of telling me something.'

Allen hesitated, there was a moment while decision hung in the balance, then he suddenly went limp. 'All right, I'll tell you what I can.'

'You recognized the body in there as that of the girl who stayed at the Marina?'

'Yes.'

'She was your girl friend?'

'You could call her that.'

'What was her name?'

'She called herself Dawn Peters but I think that was for the business . . . '

'You are willing to make a statement?'

'I've said so, haven't I?'

Wycliffe relaxed. From now on it would all be plain sailing as far as Allen was concerned. A born bully, he hadn't the guts even to be a good crook. Wycliffe stood up and went briskly to the door. 'Right! We'll get back to the station.'

The two policemen escorted Allen out and Wycliffe, after a brief word with Franks to satisfy his curiosity, followed them. It was half past twelve when they arrived back and now Wycliffe was looking at Allen with a proprietary air, he was almost jovial. 'Hungry?'

'I haven't had anything since seven this morning.'

'Take him down, see that he gets a good meal, then he can have a sleep.'

Wycliffe had decided to go back to the hotel to lunch with his wife but when he went up to the HQ room he found Gill and Fehling there.

'I think Fehling has hit upon something, sir.'

Fehling, looking sullen, like a schoolboy with a grievance, said, 'I doubt if it's of any importance but this morning, when Mr Gill told me that you suspected the money might have been intended to get Allen out of the country, it set me thinking. My mind had been on drugs but if it's a question of an illicit passage, that narrows the field. There are very few ships where you could get away with that these days.'

'Well?'

'There's a freighter alongside the Eastern breakwater, the *Peruvia*, four thousand tons, Liberian registered. She was towed in several weeks back having had a fire which badly damaged her superstructure and accommodation. She's due to sail on Monday which would have suited Allen. The girl was there with the money. . . '

'I suppose it's a line of enquiry,' Wycliffe said without much enthusiasm, 'but we shall need more than that . . . '

'There is more,' Gill cut in with impatience. 'The skipper is a Spaniard but he speaks English of a sort, and he's been seen several times lately drinking ashore with Dippy Pellow, the chap who runs one of the tender launches. And finally, when she sails on Monday, she's bound for Barranquilla.'

'Never heard of it.'

'It's the Caribbean port of Colombia.'

'And that's supposed to mean something to me?'

'It will if you read this, it's the Yard's reply to your request for further information about Allen.' He handed Wycliffe a typewritten sheet. After details of the offences for which Allen had received his various sentences, the memo went on:

Allen comes from a respectable family. His father was a schoolteacher in Surbiton. Both parents are now dead but he has a sister who married an oil engineer and is believed to be residing in Venezuela. He seems to have had no contact with his parents after . . .

Wycliffe handed back the sheet. 'Geography is not my strong point but I assume that Venezuela is next door to Colombia – is that it?'

'That, sir, is it. I suggest we have a go at that skipper and that we pull in Pellow for questioning.'

'Have a go at the skipper by all means but Pellow will keep, he can't run away.'

Wycliffe could hardly admit it but he was bored with this side of the investigation, for he was convinced that it had no direct bearing on the girl's death and that was all that interested him. Why had she been strangled? And above all, why had she been disfigured? He was on the point of telling Gill to carry on when it occurred to him that here was a chance to potter round the docks in the line of duty and there must be some privilege for rank. 'I'll see this Spanish skipper.' He was cowardly enough to add, 'Then if there's any legation trouble it will be my problem.'

Fehling's face betrayed his thoughts. 'In that case, sir, I'll be off to lunch.'

'You're coming with me, Mr Gill can eat for both of us.'

For once Fehling's petulant expression changed to a smile.

They drove through the town to the dock gates. As they passed the Marina Wycliffe wondered what Fehling would say if he suggested dropping in on them for lunch. If he could have been sure of another curry he would have been sorely tempted. On the waste ground beside Joe's café four or five articulated lorries were drawn up. 'Do you fancy something?'

'In there?'

'Why not? He does a good line in coffee with a dash of rum.'

After a moment Fehling decided to treat this as a joke. Wycliffe pulled up at the police barrier which was immediately raised. Evidently they recognized Fehling. Inside the gates he drew into the car park.

'We can drive to the ship, sir.'

'Let's walk.'

Despite the interest of the place Wycliffe almost wished that he had taken the car. Against Fehling's immense bulk he felt insignificant and as Fehling had the length of leg to go with it he found himself hopping over railway tracks, dodging hawsers and almost running to keep up. Finally he had the courage to set his own pace, which forced the inspector into line. He grinned to himself. Easy really!

It was Saturday and the place was almost deserted. They skirted the four main graving docks but Wycliffe made a small diversion to look into the basin of the largest, which housed a monstrous tanker. From the twin propellers his eye swept up over the great bulbous curve of grey steel plates to the rail towering above him. *British Emblem. London.*

'Seventy thousand tons,' Fehling said.

It was high tide and along the wharf the steeply angled gangplanks to the high riding unladen ships worried Wycliffe who had no head for heights. But the *Peruvia*, when they reached her, seemed tiny by comparison. Her renovated superstructure gleamed with fresh white paint but her hull was mottled with great splashes of red oxide where rust had been chipped off. Near the head of the gangway, which Wycliffe climbed easily, a swarthy little man in blue dungarees lent on the rail smoking. He seemed not to see them until Wycliffe addressed him. 'We are police officers and we wish to see the captain.'

The man, without moving from the rail, looked them up and down and without a word returned to his contemplation of the wharf. Fehling's reaction was swift and effective. *'Policia! Captain Hortelano immediatamente!'*

Whether it was the basic Spanish or the drill sergeant's voice and manner, the little man was galvanized into action. 'You have hidden talents, Mr Fehling,' Wycliffe observed.

'His lot have a healthy respect for the police,' Fehling confided.

They were led up a companionway to the bridge and ushered into the presence of the captain with a single word, *'Policia!'*

The captain was small and dark and sallow, a wiry little man in a dusty creased uniform with tarnished buttons and braid. His breath smelt of whisky and his speech had that special precision of enunciation which comes when a hard drinker is at a particular stage of drunkenness. His manner was ingratiating and his English good. 'You will drink with me, gentlemen?'

'No thank you.'

'That is a pity, I look for an excuse as it is not good to drink alone. All the same . . .' He fetched a bottle from a wall cupboard and poured himself a generous double.

They were in his day cabin, which was fresh from the hands of the painters, and Wycliffe had the impression that the captain was not at home in it. Perhaps he was accustomed to a cosy squalor. 'Do you carry passengers on your ship, captain?'

'Passengers? She is not a passenger ship – no. But you understand it is sometimes done that we take one or two. To keep the law they must sign as crew but they do not work and they pay. Last year we have a famous English writer and he stay with us three trips.'

'You are proposing to take a passenger when you sail on Monday?'

The captain drank half his whisky in a single swig. 'No, it was spoken of but the gentleman had not the proper papers.'

Wycliffe was standing at the curtained porthole, staring

out over the harbour; the dinghies were racing in the Roads beyond the breakwater. Fehling, monumental and immovable, stood by the door. The skipper's nervous gaze flitted from one to the other.

'The gentleman in question is under arrest.'

'So? It shows, does it not, how careful one must be?'

'You did not know that this man was wanted by the British police for robbery with violence?'

The brown eyes widened. 'But certainly I do not know! Would I ever . . . ?'

'Then why do you suppose he was going to pay a thousand pounds for his passage?'

'*Dios mi!* A thousand pounds? That Pellow – he is . . . he is *sin vergüenza*! He has talk to you, señor, but you are not correctly informed. One hundred pounds is all I was to get for this man's passage to Barranquilla. One hundred English pounds!'

Wycliffe had turned away from the porthole and he was now facing the captain. 'Perhaps you will give me the address of your owners?'

'Owners? What is this? They must not hear of this man, it was not an official arrangement, you understand, and I am in much trouble already because of the fire. If I am in more trouble my career at sea will be finish!'

Wycliffe shrugged. 'If you want to sail on Monday and you don't want your owners to know about this spot of bother, all you have to do is to tell the truth.'

'But I have told you . . . '

Wycliffe took a step towards the door. 'We'll get the address from the docks office.'

'But señor, wait!'

'Well?'

'I was to have five hundred pounds to put this man ashore in Barranquilla.'

'Without passing through immigration?'

He nodded.

'That's better. Now listen to me! If you leave the docks premises or attempt to communicate with this man Pellow or anyone else before you sail on Monday, I'll have you arrested. You understand?'

'I understand, señor. Be assured . . . '

Wycliffe strolled out on to the bridge and stood for a moment by the wheel, looking for'ard over the holds to the bow and beyond. He could see her pitching into a great wall of water, shipping it green, the decks awash, then the shuddering recovery as she began to rear like a porpoise, only to be ready for the next plunge . . .

'Captain Mac Whirr, I presume!'

'Cheeky devil! So you read Conrad?'

'I like yarns about the sea.'

Wycliffe wondered if he might have to revise his opinion of Fehling.

The docks' clock on its steel tripod, rising above the sheds, showed a quarter to two. 'Is there anywhere we can get some lunch?'

'I know a good steakhouse . . . '

'With a glass of beer?'

'At two o'clock? You must be joking!'

'Well let's make for the nearest pub and have one before we eat.'

CHAPTER EIGHT

Allen looked more composed when they brought him to Wycliffe's room in the afternoon. He sat in the chair by the desk and waited. Wycliffe stood by the window which looked out on to the blank garage wall. Detective Constable Rees, the young man to whom Wycliffe had talked that morning, installed himself in a corner with his notebook. This day had a special significance for him: he had heard much of Wycliffe's reputation and had followed all his cases; now, in a manner of speaking, they were working together. With ball-point poised he waited for the great man to begin. Wycliffe turned from the window, seemed about to sit down then changed his mind. He felt in his pocket for his pipe, brought it out, lit it, then threw over a packet of cigarettes to Allen. 'You're going to need these.' He smoked for a while then said, 'Well, my friend, I'd better caution you – you are not obliged to say anything unless you wish to . . . '

The little alarm clock on the shelf showed a quarter past three. Allen was smoking and staring at the floor. Wycliffe was moving restlessly round in the tiny space between his desk and the window, like a caged animal.

'When did you first meet her?'

'Six months ago. She was working for a group of three Soho strip clubs. You know the sort of thing – they employ a dozen or so girls who shuttle between the clubs getting in twelve or more acts apiece between two and midnight, six days a week.'

'She must have been making good money.'

Allen lit another cigarette from the stub of the old. 'Seventy-five a week.'

'What were you doing?'

Allen looked blank.

'All right! Save it! You were looking round for a likely bird who would keep you until you did your next job.'

Allen was indignant. 'What if I was? It wasn't immoral earnings!'

Wycliffe chuckled. 'There could be two opinions about that! Anyway you turned on your charm and she fell for it.'

Allen made a gesture of dissent. 'I didn't have to turn on any charm with that one, she was like a bitch in heat and after the first time I couldn't be in a room with her for five minutes before she had her pants off.'

'Where was she living?'

'She shared lodgings with another girl in Bayswater.'

'Address?'

Allen hesitated. 'I can't remember, somewhere behind Paddington Station – Sussex Place, Sussex Gardens, Sussex something . . . I could take you there.'

'You moved in?'

He shook his head. 'It wasn't on, the landlady was an interfering old bag, in any case I didn't want that . . . '

'She came to your place?'

'No, I didn't want that either; if a chap is known by his bird it gives you coppers a bit of a lever.'

'So what did you do?'

'Hotel rooms – some nights and Sundays.'

'What was she like?'

'In bed? She'd been around and she knew all the tricks.'

'And yet you hooked her.' Wycliffe wondered what the young constable was making of all this. Was this the sort of interrogation he had expected?

Allen looked modest. 'She said she never got any satisfaction from other men.'

Wycliffe did not even smile. 'Did she tell you anything about her life before she met you?'

'Not much, she said that she had worked in a club down this way.'

'Nothing else?'

Allen grinned. 'She said she was married.'

'Did she give any details?'

'She said he was an old geezer.'

'Anything else?'

'She said he was creepy.'

'What does that mean?'

Allen shrugged. 'He played with toy soldiers like a kid.'

'Why did she marry him?'

'God knows! Why do women do things?' He paused, then added, 'She said she was an orphan and I think she lived in some sort of home. She wanted to get out and this guy had money.'

'And where did this idyll take place?'

'Search me!'

Poor Willie! He had been no more than an episode in her life. Amusing to look back on, to tell her friends about. A creep who played with toy soldiers. Why had she married him? To escape from a childhood hedged in by foster parents, children's officers and the featureless omnipotence of bureaucracy. By marrying Willie she transformed herself into a woman, a woman free to explore wider horizons from a secure base. And the base served its purpose. The truth? Even as the thoughts passed through his mind he knew that they were a ludicrous over-simplification. Julie must have had her fears and her frustrations, her disappointments and her moments of bitter self reproach. Times when she felt sorry for her amiable husband and remorseful for what she was doing to him. But in the story she told, all this would be left out.

What was DC Rees thinking in his corner? Of the silences in particular? No doubt he had been told that when questioning a suspect the pressure must be kept up, never allow time for prevarication, change ground often . . . But now the suspect's eyes were closed, the room was warm and it was possible that he was dozing. The chief superintendent himself seemed near to it as he sat, elbows on the desk, his chin in his hands, staring into space.

'Was she still in these lodgings when she came down here?'

Allen opened his eyes. 'No, she'd moved to a flat.'

'Address?'

'Queensberry Mansions, Felton Terrace, Hampstead.'

'Up in the world.'

'You can say that again. She packed in with the strip joints about two months ago when she found she had a voice. Some agent took her up and she got a job in cabaret – real West End stuff . . . '

'Did you live in the flat?'

'No, she wanted me to but it suited me to carry on as before. You don't want to get in too deep with a bird.'

Wycliffe nodded as though he were in complete accord with this sentiment. 'And next thing she's staying at a crummy joint here in the far west with you on the same floor, pretending not to know her. And she gets herself murdered.' His manner changed suddenly from a lazy somnolence to vigorous aggression. 'Now, my lad, I want it straight. I know most of the story so don't try any tricks unless you want the murder rap slapped on you.'

Allen was wide enough awake now and resentful. 'I said I would talk and I will, there's no need for threats. You see, I got nicked for this wages job . . . '

'I don't want to hear about that, start from the time when you skipped.'

A moment for reorientation. 'Well, I was lucky and I got away clean. I dodged about for the rest of the day then when it was dark I made for her flat. She always said I could count on her if I was in trouble and now was her chance.'

'She knew you were bent?'

'She knew I'd done a few jobs.'

'She approved?'

He grinned. 'She seemed to get a kick out of it. She couldn't hear enough, wanted every detail. She used to egg me on, "Why don't you try something big? So far you've been taking risks for peanuts!" – that sort of talk.'

'So you went to her flat.'

'Yeh, and to give her her due, she made no bones about taking me in, she was tickled to death at the thought of the cops looking for me. I hadn't been there long when she asked me if I'd like to get out of the country. I said the chance would be a fine thing, then she said, "You told me you had a sister in Venezuela, would she take you if you could get there?" I said she would, partly because I believed it and partly because anything is better than going back inside. It may be some people's idea of a rest cure but not mine. I asked her what it was all about but she wouldn't tell me, she just said I'd be surprised at the contacts she had. Anyway, I didn't really believe her. We went on for a few days then one evening she came home and said it was all cut and dried. She told me to get a passport photo from a place down the road and some new clothes. When I was fitted out she gave me fifty quid and said I was to come down here and book in at the Marina.

I was to pretend that I was a seaman waiting for a ship and she would join me later. She told me to keep out of the way and not to let on I knew her when she arrived . . . '

'You didn't know the details of her arrangements?'

'No, she was queer like that, you had to let her make a mystery out of everything.'

'When did you arrive at the Marina?'

'I travelled down Saturday night and got there Sunday morning.'

'When did the girl arrive?'

'Sunday evening but I didn't see her until breakfast-time Monday. She didn't make any move then but she looked in my room afterwards and told me to come to her room that night round eleven. She said, "Later on I shall have company and it wouldn't do for you two to meet." '

'Well?'

Allen shifted his chair to avoid the sun which now streamed into the room from above the roof of the garage. 'Well, I went along at eleven and she told me everything was fixed. She was like a kid with a new toy – excited. She said I was to be put aboard a ship on Sunday night and that I should sail on Monday. Once outside British waters I would be treated like an ordinary passenger and on the other side they would put me ashore in Colombia with no questions asked. I should have five hundred dollars American and a passport good enough to get me across the border with Venezuela.' He lit another cigarette and inhaled deeply, starting off his cough again. When the cough had subsided he went on, 'I asked her where the money was coming from and she said that was the cream of it, her husband would pay.'

'Her husband?'

'That's what she said.'

'What happened then?'

'Happened? – nothing. I went back to my room.'

'You didn't give her a tumble to round off the evening?'

'No, she tried it on but I was in no mood for it. I'd been pretty low with bronchitis and – well, she just had to go without.'

'How did your prints come to be on the photograph in her handbag?'

'I've been thinking about that. I remember she asked me to get her handkerchief from her handbag. I saw the photo and asked her who it was.'

'Why did she carry it round?'

'Search me! She always had some man's photo in her bag, usually more than one.'

'Talking of photographs, did you notice one of her on her dressing table?'

Allen nodded. 'Yeh, in a frame, one she was fond of and carted everywhere with her.'

'When did you see her again?'

'I never did. Next day your blokes were swarming all over the place and as soon as I got the message I decided to beat it when I got the chance.'

'What were you doing in the Voodoo?'

'I had to keep off the streets and it was somewhere to go for the evening.'

'You're a liar!' Wycliffe spoke without heat. 'Do you think it was chance we picked you up as you came out?' He stood up and moved out of the sun, which was striking down exactly where he sat. 'You're not smart enough to be a crook, my lad! It would pay you to go straight. The girl arranged with the Masson-Smythes to have the thing set up for you and you thought you could go back to them and put the screw on a bit – "Look after me or else . . ." '

'That's not true!'

'Then why didn't you clear out altogether when you heard the girl had been murdered? Why hang about the town? You had twenty-four hours' start.'

'I was afraid of road checks.'

Wycliffe sighed. 'You make me tired! You're not even a good liar. What did you think when you heard that she'd been murdered?'

Allen looked at him, uncomprehending. 'I was scared – wouldn't you be? I mean, there was I on the spot, I'd been in her room and the police were already after me . . . '

Wycliffe was looking at him in detached appraisal, his stare was unnerving. In the end he made a little gesture. Impatience? Distaste? Helplessness? 'I'm going to send you back where you came from in the morning; you're no use to me. If it turns out that you did kill that girl . . . '

'I didn't kill her – why should I? I lost by it if anybody did!'

Wycliffe shook his head. 'For God's sake get him out of my sight!'

Allen sneered. 'That's the thanks you get – from cops!'

'Thanks for what?'

When they had taken him down Wycliffe stood for a long time looking out of the window and Gill found him there. 'Evening, Mr Wycliffe!'

Wycliffe did not turn round. 'I've just had a tête-à-tête with Allen. He seemed willing enough to talk about the girl but cagey on the subject of the Masson-Smythes. We want enough to put that pair inside so when Fehling comes in let him have another go at Allen – lean on him a bit.'

'I would enjoy leaning on that character myself . . . '

'No doubt, but you'll have to deprive yourself. I want you to ring the Yard, tell them we shall be returning Allen tomorrow. You can also tell them that you are coming up and that you'll need assistance.'

'To do what?'

'Contact the places she's worked at, get on to her former landlady and the neighbours in her new flat . . . Do the rounds, then ring me and tell me who did her in and why.'

Gill perched himself on the edge of Wycliffe's desk. 'When do I leave?'

'Tonight, there's a train around nine.'

'And how long have I got?'

Wycliffe turned to face him. 'Oh, don't hurry yourself, say twenty-four hours. Ring me tomorrow evening.'

Gill grinned. 'A cinch! Especially on a Sunday when London is like the Sahara desert.' He took out one of his cheroots and lit it. 'I haven't got Allen's story fitted in yet. If he's telling the truth, it was he who kept Millie awake in the next room. "Just voices", she said, "a man and a woman talking". Then she heard someone come out of the girl's room – that must have been Allen leaving. But Millie says next time she woke she heard a couple in there quarrelling and that the quarrel ended in lovemaking. We believe that the man who killed her was the man she made love with, so it couldn't have been Allen, he's the wrong blood group.' Gill broke off. 'Am I boring you, sir?'

'No, just confusing me, but carry on if you must.'

'Another visitor then. The man of the fire escape? If we believe Allen, that man could have been her husband come to deliver the money. If you ask me, it's a cock-up of a yarn. I mean, why kill your wife when you've just given her a thousand quid to help her get her lover out of the country?'

Wycliffe moved away from the window and sat at his desk. 'Get off my desk!'

Gill slid off the desk grinning. Wycliffe put his fingers together and stared at them thoughtfully. 'You have a way of making even the truth seem ridiculous, Jim. In any case, you haven't asked the most important question – how does one account for the restraint in killing and frenzied hatred suggested by the disfigurement?'

'I suppose it's possible that she was killed by one man and disfigured by another.'

'It's possible, certainly, but difficult to imagine a reason for it.'

A constable came in with a cup of tea on a tray. 'Sorry, sir, I'll fetch another cup, I didn't know the chief inspector was with you.'

'The chief inspector is leaving,' Wycliffe growled, and when the constable had gone, he went on, 'Run away, Jim. As a Dr Watson you're a dead loss and there isn't room for two Sherlocks.'

It was true, reasoned argument from Gill or from anyone else only confused him. Most of the time it hardly mattered but there came a stage in every case when it mattered a great deal. He seemed to have reached that stage now. He was like a man idly playing with a pack of cards, who finds that he has built or nearly built a clever little card house. Only two or three cards remain to be put in place and suddenly he values what he has contrived almost by accident and is afraid of spoiling it. In every difficult case in which he had eventually been successful, he had known such a time. Suddenly he would find himself in possession of a credible and convincing theory which seemed to need only a little more thought to work it out in compelling detail. It was then that he would pause, reluctant to discuss it, reluctant even to think about it.

Because his success seemed to be a matter of revelation rather than reason he had never developed any self confidence and set about every case with the feeling that this time he would be shown up at last. What an attitude of mind for a chief superintendent! He was humiliated by it and kept his self distrust a carefully guarded secret.

With Gill out of the way he felt better. He drank his tea and glanced through the reports in his tray. The Yard had sent someone to talk to the manager of Summit Theatrical Costumiers, the firm whose name appeared on the scrap of paper found in Allen's room with the address of the Marina scribbled on it. 'Yes, we have business dealings with Thelma Masson-Smythe at the Voodoo' . . . 'Yes, all the firm's letters are signed by me with the carbon in place.' Carbon copies of the correspondence with the Voodoo were produced and the fragment was found to match with the carbon copy of a letter dated 17th June regarding a disputed account. The carbon copy was being forwarded.

A bit of evidence linking the Masson-Smythes with Allen which might be useful if either or both persisted in denying the connection. It was obvious that the girl had sent him to the Voodoo and that he had been sent from there to the Marina.

Another of the reports also concerned the Masson-Smythes. They had been questioned about Allen's presence in the club and denied all knowledge of him. 'He is not a member, of course, but unfortunately it is all too easy for non-members to gate-crash . . . No, I've never seen him before.' Acting on instructions, the detective had seemed to accept this assurance without question. 'I hope he was convincing,' Wycliffe muttered. He wanted Allen's statement before he took any action against the Masson-Smythes and he thought that Fehling could be persuasive enough to make it good. He pushed the reports back into the tray and decided to spend the evening with his wife. He felt relaxed again.

He decided to walk, and not far from the station, by the Catholic Church, he almost collided with a woman coming out of the presbytery. She was vaguely familiar, tall and gaunt, wearing a severely tailored black costume and a black toque. Aunt Jane. He was sure that she had not recognized him, in fact, she had probably not even seen him and he could have sworn that her eyes were red with crying. He watched her stepping it out across the square. He wondered what secrets she had been whispering to her priest.

At the corner of Castle Hill a man selling newspapers, and a poster against the wall: *Moonlanding tonight?* He bought a paper and sharing the front page with the Apollo XI astronauts was a smudgy reproduction of Julie's photograph. The face looked back at him, the lips parted in a faint smile, the eyes wide and frank. Both Kathy and Piper had said that the photograph was 'like her' but that there was something not quite right about it. Could it be that the restoration gave her a look of innocence? It was his belief that satisfying sexual experience leaves its mark on the face of a girl. He could not define it but he thought that he knew it when he saw it and he had once called it the Mona Lisa smirk.

'Good evening, superintendent!' It was the little red-headed reporter. 'So you know who she was.'

Wycliffe wagged the paper. 'It doesn't say so here.'

'I write the stuff, I don't read it. What I can't understand is why you've been so coy about publishing the photograph. I could have told you who she was quick enough and so could a good many others in this town.'

'We had a good reason.'

'I suppose I could try the dailies with that.'

'With what?'

'Detective Chief Superintendent Wycliffe told our reporter that the police had good reason for withholding publication of the dead girl's photograph! A nasty-minded editor might smell a rat and come to the conclusion that somebody was getting the blanket treatment.'

Wycliffe laughed. 'What's the time?'

Brown looked at his watch. 'Just gone six.'

'Come and have a drink.'

The pub in Castle Hill backed on to the harbour; in fact, the main bar was built out on stilts so that at high tide it seemed to be afloat. They were the only customers. Wycliffe ordered two beers and carried them to the window seat at the far end of the room. They were close to the quay where the pleasure boats unloaded and at this time the boats were nuzzling each other for positions close to the steps. The passengers from less aggressive ones had to climb over two or even three other boats to reach the steps, but it was all part of the fun. And it was all as stale to the reporter as it was novel to Wycliffe. Brown sipped his beer.

'Now, young man!' Wycliffe ruffled through the papers in his briefcase and came out with one of the photographs taken by the police photographer of the injuries to the dead girl's face. 'Would you have identified her from that?'

Brown gave the photograph one glance and turned away. 'Christ!'

'Exactly. That was all we had to go on.'

Brown was white and for a moment Wycliffe thought he was going to be sick. 'Are you all right?'

'I suppose so. But nobody ever said that . . . '

'No, we deliberately kept quiet about that but it doesn't matter now. I intend to make a statement to the press on Monday. But if you jump the gun . . .!'

'You can rely on me.'

'I hope so. Now, I want something from you. Tell me about the Collinses.'

The reporter was recovering his poise. 'It makes a change being interviewed.'

'You're not being interviewed, my lad, you're being interrogated and don't you forget it.'

'OK. Have it your way. You've met them?'

'I've met them.'

'Well, you know what they're like. Everybody thought that Willie would end up by marrying the woman who does the books . . . ' He snapped his fingers in an effort to recall a name. 'Rogers – Iris Rogers. And she would have taken on where mother left off, if you see what I mean.'

Wycliffe nodded.

'People in the town used to say, "I wonder how much longer poor old Iris will have to wait" – of course they all knew that it would be until the old lady kicked the bucket.'

'The old lady is the boss?'

'You can say that again! Unless Willie was the product of a virgin birth, which wouldn't surprise me, there must have been a father round sometime but not in my day. Of course, the Collinses have got money – real money and it would be worth waiting for.'

'But he married Julie.'

Brown chuckled. 'It was a nine days' wonder – a kid of eighteen and a real doll at that! I mean, everybody wondered what he was going to do to her and what he was going to do it with . . . '

'You confine yourself to the facts, young man!'

'Sorry! I thought you wanted atmosphere, it must be the journalist in me. She was an orphan or something and as I remember it there was nobody at the wedding from her side except the foster mother.'

'Church?'

'You bet! With all the cake and trimmings, a real "do" for the town to gawp at and gossip about. Reception at the Royal.' He grinned. 'Even Aunt Jane was there.'

'Was that surprising?'

'I'll say! Aunt Jane is RC and she thinks the established church is the antichrist. They're a jolly family.'

'How long did Julie stay with them?'

'Six months, maybe. Even before that there was talk.'

'What sort of talk?'

Brown lit a cigarette and considered. 'After the excitement of the wedding had died down it all went quiet for a month or two, she was even helping in the shop and to everybody's surprise it looked as though it might work. Then she started living it up a bit; there's a country club on the Truro road and she was there most nights.'

'With her husband?'

'You must be joking! Anyway it wasn't long before she was involved in a car smash. She wasn't hurt but the driver was. It was Masson-Smythe, the chap at the Voodoo. I suppose he wanted to keep out of trouble with his wife so he said she'd thumbed a lift in the rain and he'd felt sorry for her. Could even have been true but it didn't make any difference to the gossip.'

'Anybody else?'

The reporter drained his glass. 'Have another?'

'No thanks. I asked you if there was anybody else?'

'There was plenty of talk but the only other name named, so to speak, was a chap called Byrne, a schoolteacher at the Greville Road Comprehensive.'

'Then she left him?'

Brown nodded. 'It was rumoured that she'd gone away with Byrne, I lost track of her, then at the beginning of last season she turned up doing her striptease at the

Voodoo. I reckon she did it deliberately and it was bloody cruel. I mean, in this town . . . '

Wycliffe stood up. 'You'll keep quiet about all this?'

Brown grinned. 'You're the boss, but you'll owe me something for Wednesday's issue.'

'It will be all over by then.'

'You're serious?'

Almost to his own surprise Wycliffe decided that he was. They left the pub together. Outside Brown had a final go. 'You'll be seeing Willie tonight?'

Wycliffe looked at him poker-faced. 'The shop's closed for the week-end.'

'Madame is in the Television Lounge, superintendent.'

Since his identity had become known he had received VIP treatment at the hotel and he hated it. He didn't know how to behave; in his anxiety not to appear patronizing he thought that he was probably churlish. All the same, the man called after him, 'A moment, if you please, sir!' The porter was holding a little book. 'Perhaps you will be kind enough to sign my boy's autograph, sir?'

Wycliffe took the book and scrawled his signature.

'And write Detective Chief Superintendent, if you will, sir.'

He found Helen in the television room watching a report on the astronauts. The room was fairly full and all heads turned to look as he came in. 'They put on a photograph of the girl who was murdered and they had one of you on too – one I haven't seen before. You looked as though . . . '

He sat watching the television until dinner time and after dinner they took their coffee out on to the terrace where the light was fading into warm, intimate summer darkness. It was a time for mellowness and ease but he was restless.

After he had lighted his pipe twice and put it out again, Helen asked, 'Why don't you ring the station?'

He pretended not to understand but after a while he said, 'I think I'll take a stroll before bed.'

'I'll expect you when I see you.'

CHAPTER NINE

He did not consciously direct his steps but without any clear idea in his mind about what he would do, he found himself outside the bookshop. Several of the shops in the street had their windows brilliantly lit, the florist's opposite, for example, had a window full of flowers cleverly lit from below and kept fresh by a fine spray which made rainbows in the light. But the bookshop was in total darkness, the old-fashioned blue canvas blinds were down. Looking up, he thought he could see a faint glimmer of light coming from the sitting room of the flat, one of the rooms which overlooked the street.

What were they doing? Was Willie in his room with his soldiers? Was he thinking of Julie? Wycliffe felt guilty; to confront him with the hideously mutilated features of his wife without warning was an act of cruelty. No wonder he had collapsed. In his own way he had deeply loved the schoolgirl to whom his mother had married him. At least he had loved the image he made of her.

What puzzled Wycliffe was his attitude afterwards. He had made no protest and seemed to bear no animosity against the superintendent, yet there had been a change in him not entirely explicable in terms of shock. At first Wycliffe could not make out what it was, then he decided that it was anger, cold anger, suppressed and dangerous. But against whom?

'I'm sorry that I had to submit you to that but it was necessary.'

No answer.

'You realize that your wife was dead before that was done to her?'

'Yes.'

'Have you any idea who could have done it?'

'No.'

'You are sure?'

'Quite sure!'

And that was all. Now he had to probe the wound.

He looked at his watch: a quarter to ten. Perhaps the two women were already in bed. When Julie was there they had played three-handed bridge. What did they do now?

He opened the door of the side passage which ran beside the shop. Almost at the far end there was a door in the left hand wall and a small light over a bell-push which shone on a printed card: *COLLINS. PRIVATE*. He rang the bell. Almost at once he was startled by a woman's voice from close at hand. A speak-box which he hadn't expected. He found the little metal grille and spoke into it.

'Come up, please.'

He opened the door and went up the carpeted stairs, past the green baize door to the bookroom and on up the next flight to the flat. The musty smell of the books pervaded everything. It was Miss Rogers who waited for him on the top landing – Iris, the reporter called her. She was tight lipped. 'You didn't waste much time getting here.'

'I beg your pardon?'

'It's barely ten minutes since Dr Rashleigh phoned you – or at least, he phoned the station.'

'What's the trouble?'

She looked surprised. 'Didn't he tell you?' She sniffed. 'As he was so anxious to drag in the police he'd better tell you himself. He's in the sitting room.'

In the dimly lit room where the brown velvet curtains met and overlapped across the window, Dr Rashleigh stood, elegant, yet restless and incongruous. He seemed relieved to see Wycliffe. 'So you've come yourself. I asked them to tell you but I didn't expect you to come. I don't want to make too much of this but I thought that in view of everything it would be better . . . '

'What exactly has happened?'

'She tried to poison herself it seems.'

'Who?'

Rashleigh looked impatient. 'Why, Aunt Jane, of course! Miss Collins.' Evidently the Collinses were such an established institution in the town that even this rather pompous doctor found it natural to speak of them with familiarity.

'What did she use?'

'Strychnine.'

'A pretty sure method.'

'As a rule, but not this time. She'll be up and about again tomorrow.'

'She's in hospital?'

'I thought it wiser for the night.'

Wycliffe sat down on one of the low armchairs and rested his head back against the embroidered runner. 'Tell me about it.' He got out his pipe and started to fill it. 'You said just now, "She tried to poison herself, it *seems*", – is there any doubt about it?'

Rashleigh looked distastefully at the other armchairs and chose instead a straight-backed dining chair. 'This *is* a depressing room, don't you think? Every time I come here . . . ' His voice trailed off, then he added in a burst of confidence, 'I've been coming to this house for twenty-five years and in all that time I don't think they've moved so much as an ornament!'

It was obvious that he was talking himself into more relevant disclosures. He fiddled with the perfect crease in the fine herringbone tweed of his trousers. It was difficult to credit that perhaps an hour earlier he was wrestling with a case of strychnine poisoning. 'I very much doubt if she intended to kill herself, superintendent. In fact, I strongly suspect that the effect of the strychnine she took was more than she'd bargained for, poor lady.'

'Then why did she take it at all?'

Rashleigh examined the long tapering fingers of a pale hand. 'Some people, especially women who are starved of . . . of affection, feel compelled to draw attention to themselves by some means, however drastic.'

Wycliffe felt like making a rude noise. 'You mean that she's tried it before?'

Rashleigh frowned. 'About three years ago; it was an overdose of a barbiturate which I had prescribed for her insomnia. On that occasion I persuaded her to enter a nursing home for a period.'

'A mental home?'

Rashleigh nodded unhappily. 'Yes.'

'Where did she get the strychnine?'

'Apparently it has been in the house for years, they had it for poisoning rats in the cellar. These old houses by the harbour . . . '

'Why did you send for me?'

Rashleigh bristled. 'I didn't *send* for you!'

'All right, why did you want me to be told?'

The doctor straightened his Greyhounds tie. 'One hears rumours. There must be few people in this town who have not heard that the girl murdered at the Marina was Collins's wife.'

Wycliffe had to acknowledge the truth of that. Kenny the Man, the Masson-Smythes, Sadie, the reporter, not to mention the Collinses themselves; somebody was bound to talk. But he was wilfully obtuse. 'You think that there may be a connection between the murder and this?'

'Certainly not!' Rashleigh was shocked. 'No direct connection that is. The emotional disturbance could well have been the trigger. With an unstable personality . . . '

'But do you discount entirely the possibility that Aunt Jane was poisoned by someone else?'

The doctor stood up to lend emphasis to his disclaimer. 'My dear superintendent! The very idea is unthinkable!'

'Who found her?'

Rashleigh smiled. 'You do not have to *find* someone suffering from strychnine poisoning. She was in her bedroom and her cries were heard by everyone in the flat – by Willie and his mother and by Iris Rogers.'

'What was *she* doing here?'

'You will be able to ask her that question yourself.'

It was odd, the more meticulous and precise the person he had to deal with the more abrupt and boorish his manner was apt to become. It was almost a reflex response. He invited snubs from such people and seemed oblivious of them. In fact, it was an aspect of his own sensitivity. In the presence of fastidiousness he felt that he and his job were being mutely criticized.

'I would like to see her bedroom.'

Rashleigh led the way. The room was next to the sitting room and, like it, overlooked the narrow street. It was large and sparsely furnished; an old-fashioned wooden single bed with slatted head and foot, a wardrobe, a chest of drawers and a table across the window which to judge from the few trinkets on it served as a dressing table. By the bed a small table held a reading lamp and several devotional books. Above the bed, a crucifix. The carpet was threadbare and the bedclothes lay on it in a twisted heap.

'She suffered convulsions, of course, but they were not excessively violent. I administered pentathol intravenously with success.'

Wycliffe looked round the room, bewildered at the perversity of human nature. Here was a woman, no more than middle aged, well-off, by no means stupid . . . He muttered to himself, 'It's masochistic!'

Rashleigh looked at him brightly. 'Isn't it?'

The tumbler was on the mantelpiece next to a plated alarm clock. Wycliffe picked it up; damp white crystals adhered to the sides and there was a similar sediment in the bottom. 'There must be enough here to kill an elephant!'

'There is, but it doesn't dissolve very easily in water, fortunately. She actually got very little down, I imagine.'

'But how do you know that she didn't intend . . . '

'I know my patient.'

'Where did you find the tumbler?'

'It had rolled under the bed.'

'How long after the call before you arrived here, doctor?'

'Not more than ten minutes. I was in my surgery as she well knew that I should be.'

Smug bastard! But he was probably right. 'She was conscious when you arrived?'

'Fully, but she said very little – just kept repeating the words, "God forgive me! God forgive me!" whenever the spasms allowed her to speak.'

'Where are the others?'

The doctor shrugged. 'Willie went to his room, I suppose that he is still there.'

'With his soldiers.'

A faint smile.

'And his mother?'

'Mrs Collins was somewhat excited. I gave her a sedative and she is sleeping.'

Wycliffe fiddled with the trinkets on the dressing table: a cameo brooch, a rosary, a locket . . . He sighed and became, abruptly, almost genial. He thanked the doctor for his cooperation and began to edge him out on to the landing.

'Good night, doctor! I expect that you can find your own way out.'

When Rashleigh had put on his hat and coat, collected his case and departed, Wycliffe stood in the passage outside Willie's door. He had his hand on the knob. In any other household . . . Then he changed his mind and went on down the passage to the kitchen. The door was open and the light was on.

'Here I am, superintendent.' Iris was standing just inside the kitchen door. Had she been eavesdropping? If so she was entirely composed.

The kitchen had been modern in the thirties; a mottled enamel gas cooker and washboiler, a refrigerator with a lot of polished wood in its structure. But everything shone, and, as a bonus, the kitchen overlooked the harbour. The curtains were undrawn and he could see, vaguely, the outline of boats in the darkness.

'I thought you might want to talk to me.'

'Yes.'

'We could go to the sitting room.'

'I like kitchens,' Wycliffe said, which was true.

They sat on cane chairs placed on opposite sides of a large, square, scrubbed table, just like the one that had taken up most of the room in his mother's kitchen. Iris looked out of place in her severely cut two-piece and her no-nonsense blouse. She belonged to an office as surely as a typewriter or a filing cabinet. Wycliffe had known scores like her, hardworking, dependable, their one satisfaction in life being indispensable. She was not bad looking, big boned with a tendency to fleshiness, but her features were good. A slightly pinched look round the nostrils might mean a shrewish temper and when the light caught her at a certain angle it was possible to see golden hairs on her upper lip. Her hair was straw coloured and her skin freckled.

'I want you to know where I stand . . . ' He could have forecast the opening. 'I've worked in this business for sixteen years.'

'A long time.'

She nodded. 'But there's more to it than that; if it hadn't been for that girl – Julie – I should have been married to him by now. I thought that it was better for you to hear it from me rather than from gossip.'

'Are you trying to tell me that you had a motive for the murder?' He couldn't resist provoking her.

She was contemptuous. 'Don't be absurd, I merely wanted you to have your facts right.'

'Thank you. Now, what do you know about this evening's business?'

She reached into her handbag, which lay open on the table, and drew out a silver cigarette case and a lighter to match. 'Smoke?' Wycliffe refused and she lit a cigarette but the hand holding the lighter trembled. Evidently she had less self possession than she liked to admit. 'If you think this affair tonight has anything to do with Julie's death then you're barking up the wrong tree. Aunt Jane is queer in the head – she's done this sort of thing before but she's no intention of killing herself.'

'Then why pretend? It's a hazardous business.'

Iris blew out a thin spiral of smoke and watched it rise. 'She did it to bring Willie to heel.'

'I don't understand.'

She looked at him doubtfully. 'Have you ever seen them together – Willie and his aunt?'

'I have.'

'Then you must have noticed. She dotes on him, it's

pathological. To her, he's the son she's never had and the man she's never married.'

Wycliffe smiled faintly. He took out his half smoked pipe and asked permission to light it. 'What about tonight?'

She reached a saucer from the dresser to do duty as an ashtray. 'There was a row, I don't know what about. On Saturday nights I stay on late to square up the books for the week. I'd finished downstairs and when I came up to the flat as usual to tell Willie I was going, she was outside his door begging him to let her in. She was crying.'

'What happened?'

'When she saw me she went to her own room. I called to Willie to let me in and he did. He was obviously very upset but I couldn't get out of him what it was about. It was while I was with him that she started to scream.'

Wycliffe was watching her with a mild fixity of expression, almost as though his thoughts were elsewhere and when he spoke it was to say something not directly relevant. 'You would have married Mr Collins if . . .?'

'If I'd had the chance – yes.' She stubbed out her cigarette in the saucer with a vigorous jab.

'The match he made seems to have been unfortunate.'

'Unfortunate! It was absurd and disastrous!'

'One would have thought that his mother and his aunt would have persuaded him . . . '

'They encouraged him! At least his mother did.'

'Indeed?'

'Yes. That seems odd to you, doesn't it? But she had a good reason – to stop him marrying me.'

'Mrs Collins disapproved of you?'

Her nostrils looked more pinched now and there were spots of colour in her cheeks. 'As a daughter-in-law, yes. She knew that once I was Willie's wife things would be different. I'm no teen-aged girl to dance to her tune. In her eyes, Willie's interest in Julie was an answer to a prayer, a young girl, an orphan, who could be brought up in the way she should go. With her, "Yes, Mrs Collins, No, Mrs Collins, It's very kind of you, Mrs Collins", the old lady thought that butter wouldn't melt in her mouth. For once, she was wrong!' Iris lit a second cigarette and smoked rapidly, making the tobacco glow and crackle and expelling the smoke in bursts. As Wycliffe watched her he was mildly perturbed at the antagonism he felt towards her. Surely she had the right to be resentful?

'How did he first meet the girl?'

'She used to come to the shop – into the secondhand department. At first she came with other girls and I think they did it for a lark, there used to be a lot of giggling, but the rest soon got tired of it and she came alone. She was at the grammar school doing "A" levels in history and English and, to give her her due, I think she had a genuine feeling for books. She soon got talking to Willie, who is more of a scholar than a business man, and he used to help her with her essays and advise her on her reading. Of course she was flattered by the attention of an older man and it was a novel experience for Willie to have a pretty young girl with auburn hair and violet eyes hanging on his every word. Of course, she saw her chance . . . '

'Are you saying that she set out to . . . '

'To seduce him – certainly she did!'

'A man double her age?'

She made a little contemptuous noise with her lips. 'You men are all the same, even policemen who should know better! You'll never believe that young girls can be truly wicked – certainly not the ones with a pretty face and nice legs. You should have seen this one go to work! "You make me feel so stupid! It's all crystal clear when you explain it. If you were a teacher . . . I feel so guilty, wasting your time like this . . . " And on another tack: "I suppose I've had a sad life, really . . . I often wonder . . . if my parents hadn't been killed. Daddy was a painter . . . " Actually daddy was a carpenter and they were taking their first holiday abroad – Majorca, I think it was, but she made it sound as though they took planes as we take buses.'

'She seems to have fooled Mrs Collins successfully, a difficult feat if I'm any judge.' Wycliffe was cool.

'She was taken in because she wanted to be!' Iris was more at her ease now. 'Of course you are writing off most of what I say on the grounds that I'm a frustrated old maid, a bit warped and more than a bit spiteful. Up to a point you may be right but there's more to it than that. As I said, I've worked in this business for sixteen years and without any false modesty I've saved it from the fate of most bookshops in towns of this size. I felt I had a stake in the place and I didn't see why I should be cheated of it by a scheming chit of a girl!'

Wycliffe looked at the chin, the set of the jaw and the pursed lips. 'The marriage lasted only a few months and it is two years since she left him – a year since she left the town altogether. During that time have you resumed your old relationship?'

She stubbed out her cigarette butt. 'Obviously we couldn't get married.'

'He had grounds for divorce.'

For some reason she flushed and shook her head. 'He wouldn't – at least . . . '

'What were you going to say?'

She hesitated. 'I was going to say that his attitude seemed to be changing in recent months. Given time I think he might have agreed, then she came back . . . '

Whether she realized it or not she was gilding the lily as far as motive went. She had reason enough to kill but surely not in the particular way that Julie died?

'And now that she is dead?'

She looked up angrily and seemed on the point of protesting but changed her mind. 'I don't know. I don't know anything any more.'

Wycliffe smoked in silence for a while. 'Before he met his wife, were you engaged?'

'No, there was an understanding, I told you.'

'What does that mean?'

'I don't know what you're asking me.'

'Did you go to bed with him?'

Again the colour flooded her cheeks. 'Yes.'

'And now?'

Her reply was barely audible. 'Yes.' She made an angry movement. 'What does that make me?'

'I don't know. Compassionate or determined, it depends on your motive.'

She looked at him sharply but said nothing. Wycliffe sat with his elbows on the table and for at least two minutes the silence was unbroken except for the ticking of the kitchen clock. 'What has been the effect on Willie of his wife's death?'

She leaned back in her chair, more relaxed. 'I wish I knew. I can't understand him. I mean, he knew that she was dead on Wednesday and of course he was upset – desperately upset, but he was normal, if you know what I mean. He was just as you might expect him to be . . . '

'But now?'

'Since you were here yesterday he's changed. I can't explain it but it frightens me. I mean, he's doing all the usual things and when you speak to him he answers you quite sensibly, but you get the impression he isn't really there at all. He's like a man walking in his sleep but I can't find out what it is.'

'He won't discuss it with you?'

'No.'

'You know that I took him to identify his wife's body?'

'Yes, but seeing her shouldn't have affected him like that, surely?'

Wycliffe reached for his briefcase and took out the photograph of the dead girl's face. He placed it on the table within her reach. 'That may explain it.'

She took the photograph and glanced at it. 'My God! You let him see that!'

'The girl was murdered, that's all that matters to me – murdered and mutilated after death.'

'Whoever did that must be mad!' She shuddered involuntarily then went quiet, 'You don't think that he . . . '

'How do I know what to think?'

'But Willie couldn't! I mean violence of any sort appalls him. He's gentle . . . ' She stopped, looking at Wycliffe. 'Nothing I can say will make any difference, will it?'

He shrugged.

After a while she got up. 'I'd better go.'

'No.'

She looked at him in surprise but sat down again.

'Does the old lady suffer from heart trouble?'

'Why, yes . . . '

'Serious?'

'I suppose so, the doctor says any sudden shock might kill her. Actually I think she's shock proof except where Willie is concerned.'

'What about Aunt Jane?'

His manner was different, more relaxed. The way he said 'Aunt Jane' almost made her laugh. 'She's as strong as a horse.'

'Any insanity in the family?'

She became guarded once more. 'Well, you know about

Aunt Jane – whether you call that insanity I don't know.'

'And?'

She fiddled with the clasp of her bag. 'Willie's father died in the asylum but that was before I started to work here.' She looked across at Wycliffe meeting his placid gaze. 'I know what you're thinking, but Willie is as sane as you or me.'

'When did you first hear that Julie had been murdered?'

She became obviously agitated. 'I heard about the murder Wednesday lunchtime but I didn't know that it was her.'

'Who told you that it was?'

She hesitated. 'I heard it from somebody yesterday – after you'd been.'

'You're a bad liar!'

She stood up, flushed and angry. 'I'm leaving!'

'No!' His manner startled her. 'I'm conducting a murder inquiry, Miss Rogers, and I will not listen to fairy tales. Please sit down and answer my questions truthfully. When did you first hear that Julie was back in town?'

'I don't know what you're talking about.'

He leaned forward in his chair and spoke confidentially. 'If you are frank now you may save yourself a great deal of embarrassment later. You have already told me – perhaps unwittingly – that Mr Collins and, by implication, you also, knew on Wednesday that it was Julie who had been murdered. Now I want to know when it was you heard that she had come back?'

She gave in and sat down. 'I saw her just as she got off the coach on Sunday evening when I was on my way home from church.'

'Where do you live?'

She gestured vaguely. 'Up on the terraces, I have a flat.'

'Alone?'

'Yes.'

'Did Julie see you?'

'I'm sure she didn't; she was getting her luggage from the boot of the coach and talking to the driver.'

'But you had no doubt that it was she?'

'I'd know her anywhere.'

'How did you find out that she was staying at the Marina?'

'I followed her.'

'She took a taxi.'

'So did I – from the same rank.'

'Why?'

'Because I wanted to know where she was going. I've never made the mistake of underestimating her ability to cause trouble.'

'Didn't it strike you as odd that she should stay at a place like the Marina?'

'I couldn't understand it.'

'You told Willie you'd seen her?' It was inevitable that he would drop into the habit of calling them all by their intimate family names.

'I rang him as soon as I got home, it seemed the natural thing to do.'

'Of course, what was his reaction?'

She hesitated. 'It's difficult to say.'

'You mean that he seemed to know already?'

She looked steadily at the table top and said nothing. He could see that she was close to tears and tears did not come easily to her. He stood up and went to the window to give her a moment to recover. Not much to be seen, just the shadowy outlines of the moored craft and the shimmering paths of their riding lights. 'Did you expect Julie to leave him?'

He heard her stifle a sob. 'I didn't know at first, I wasn't sure what she was prepared to give up. Then she started going out in the evenings and there were rumours about one or two men . . . '

'Masson-Smythe?'

'Smythe first, he runs the club where she went to work in the end, then there was a schoolteacher called Byrne.' She shook herself as though to rid her body of some cloying contact. 'Can you understand a girl like that? It was Byrne she went off with but it only lasted a week or two.' She laughed. 'Not even a long hot summer. Then she was back again.'

'You saw her go into the Marina on Sunday evening, was that the last you saw of her?'

'Yes.'

'Did you or Willie mention her again?'

'No.'

'Not even when you heard about the murder?'

'Well, yes. I heard about the murder from a customer. Willie had been at the printing works all the morning and when he came back, I said, "Was it her?" He was as white as death and he just said, "Yes".'

'Nothing more?'

She shook her head. 'He burst out crying.'

Wycliffe stood for a while, apparently lost in thought. Actually, though ideas chased each other through his mind they could hardly be said to have any pattern of rational consecutive thought. A mother's boy at thirty-six finds himself in love, probably for the first time in his life. The man on the fire escape – who was he? What did he see? Group AB? A question easily answered – too easily; he wasn't ready for that yet. He had once shocked a subordinate by saying, 'I like to have a theory before I get lumbered with too many facts!' Now the story was often told against him, but it was true. In this case he wanted to get the psychology right before he blundered into accusations of guilt. Could Willie have battered his dead wife's features into an unrecognizable tangle of skin and flesh and bone? Wycliffe felt sure that if he had killed his wife it was an unpremeditated crime – 'almost accidental' he had said to Gill. The restraint in the killing, the violence of the disfigurement – he kept coming back to it. Fear? Who else would need or want to disfigure the girl?

He was half surprised to find himself still in the kitchen with Iris sitting at the table watching him. The clock showed five minutes to eleven. It was beginning to rain, he could see the water beginning to run down the window panes, playing tricks with the harbour lights. 'Is there much cash kept in the flat or in the shop?'

The question surprised her. 'Some nights there may be as much as three or four hundred pounds in the safe in my office.'

'That money is in your charge?'

'Of course.' She added, 'Willie has a key.'

'Are cheques drawn on the business account signed by Willie alone?'

'They are not signed by Willie at all, the business belongs to his mother for her lifetime and she signs the cheques.'

'What about Aunt Jane?'

Iris bridled. 'It has nothing whatever to do with her!'

'But surely she must have shared in her father's will?'

'She was left certain investments which, by all accounts, have done very well for her.'

'Well, thank you Miss Rogers, you've been very helpful.'

'You're going?'

'Yes.'

'You're not seeing Willie?'

'Not tonight.'

She seemed reluctant to let him go. 'I hope that I haven't given you the impression . . . ' She saw the look on his face and stopped. 'All right, I'm on the telephone at home as well as here. If you want me . . . '

'Yes.' He hesitated. 'Will the old lady be all right in the house with only Willie?'

Iris smiled. 'I've been thinking about that, perhaps I'd better stay here tonight.'

He decided to look in at the station on his way back to the hotel. To his surprise he found Fehling in the HQ room, his bulk squeezed into one of the bentwood armchairs, busy writing. 'Still here? Any progress with Allen?'

Fehling's satisfaction was unmistakable. 'He's made a fresh statement, sir.'

'Involving the Masson-Smythes?'

'Up to the neck! The girl sent him to the Masson-Smythes and they made the arrangements. This fellow Pellow is their go-between with the ships and he's done similar jobs before. Allen isn't very bright and when the girl was killed he panicked and went there.'

'Good!'

Wycliffe stood by the window watching the rain. A constable came in and began to collect dirty teacups from among the litter on the tables. Outside the rain was falling vertically, thin threads that gleamed in the light of the street lamps. The square was almost deserted, a single taxi on the rank, a man and a girl under one umbrella hurrying home. He turned to Fehling. 'It's time you got some sleep, Mr Fehling, but there are a couple of things I'd like you to lay on tomorrow. Pick up Dippy Pellow, quietly, without making a fuss. With Allen's statement and what you get from him, you should have enough to book him. Make sure the Voodoo is kept under observation but don't bring the Masson-Smythes in unless they try to make a bolt for it. One more thing, fix it so that Kathy Johnson can see Masson-Smythe without him knowing. I want to see if she recognizes him.'

'Anything else, Mr Wycliffe?'

Wycliffe was wandering aimlessly round the room as though loath to leave. 'What? Oh, no! Have a good night.'

He went down the stairs and out of the front door into the rain, his shoulders hunched, and by the time he reached his hotel he was soaked to the skin.

CHAPTER TEN

Wycliffe hoped that Sunday would prove uneventful and that he would have time to think. After breakfast – nine o'clock on Sundays – he went out on to the terrace to smoke his first pipe of the day. He was on his own – Helen had made friends with some local people who had a motor launch and she was going with them across the bay to explore a bit of Daphne du Maurier country. He could have gone with them but though he intended to have a lazy day his conscience would not allow him to break contact for eight or nine hours. In any case it was pleasant on the terrace. The sky was deep blue with fleecy white clouds and at dozens of moorings peppered all over the harbour boat owners were bailing out, scrubbing down, checking motors or rigging – whatever they were doing it seemed to be delectable employment to Wycliffe. Nearby a boy and a girl were cooking breakfast on a bottle-gas stove on the deck of a little sailing craft. They must have been hard put even to sleep in the tiny cabin. The boy wore shorts and the girl a bikini. Wycliffe secretly wished that he could have his youth over again in this permissive society on which so much is blamed. It looked good enough to him that morning.

He sat in one of the wicker chairs and read the two glossy Sundays, mostly about Apollo XI, until the church bells started ringing. One, close by, a cracked bell, tolled so rapidly that it imparted a sense of urgency to its message while across the water a more melodious cadence nicely countered its monotony. Sunday: there was something in the air at the same time relaxing and inhibiting. Because of his Methodist upbringing he associated it with the smell of pitch pine pews and hymn books. When the bar opened he had a drink brought to him on the terrace.

'Excuse me . . . Superintendent Wycliffe? . . . My name is Byrne . . . '

A stockily built young man, fair haired with a good-natured, not very intelligent face, and rugby player written all over him. 'It's about the photograph in the newspaper – I knew the girl . . . ' He loomed over Wycliffe, standing first on one leg then on the other.

'Pull up a chair. Drink?'

'What? – No thank you . . . yes, I think I will, a beer if I may . . . '

Wycliffe signalled the waiter. The terrace was getting busy with people who wanted to get in some drinking time before lunch. They sat watching the harbour while they waited for the drinks. The young couple from the sailing boat were swimming now, chasing each other in the water and laughing. Byrne looked miserable, *la dolce vita* had landed him where he was now. The waiter came back with his beer and a whisky for Wycliffe.

'Cheers!'

'Cheers!'

Wycliffe put down his glass, his grey eyes on the young man. 'You went off with her, stayed with her about three weeks, then came back without her. Now let's have the details.'

Byrne looked relieved by this approach, he relaxed. 'I met her at a Rugby Club dance.'

'Are you married?'

'I am now but I wasn't then.' He hesitated. 'I want to keep my wife out of this if it can be managed. She's Welsh and just a bit . . . '

'Go on.'

'Well, I know it sounds odd but she made a bee line for me. You'd have thought I was the only man in the room.'

'She must like 'em stocky,' Wycliffe muttered, remembering Allen.

'Pardon?'

'Never mind!'

'Afterwards I wanted to take her home but she said that wasn't on.'

'Did you know who she was?'

'No, not then. Anyway, she asked me if I lived with my parents and I said I didn't, I had a flat. I must admit I was a bit taken aback when she said, "That's all right then, I'll take *you* home".' He looked out over the water. 'I suppose I was still a bit wet behind the ears but I couldn't make her out; I wondered if I'd picked up a pro without knowing it.'

'What happened?'

He turned his frank blue eyes on Wycliffe. 'I never knew a girl could be like that! And yet she was so small and so . . . ' He fumbled for a word.

'Exquisite.'

He agreed at once. 'Yes, that's the word for her – exquisite and yet she was like . . . like . . . Well, I suppose every man has sort of sex fantasies. I mean he never expects them to come true, he never expects to find a woman who . . . But she *insisted* . . . ' He broke off, at a loss for words to describe his relationship with the girl. The language of eroticism is limited and follows a tricky path between mere clinical description and obscenity.

'So you owe her something?'

He looked at the superintendent suspecting a joke but the grey eyes were serious. 'Owe her something?'

'For helping to make a man of you. You are probably a better husband because of her.'

He looked surprised. 'Yes, I suppose so, I'd never thought of it like that.'

Wycliffe emptied his glass. 'You continued to see her and finally took her away with you although, by then, you must have known that she was a married woman. Did you intend to go for good?'

Byrne felt that in some way the question was loaded against him and he bungled his answer. 'For good? I don't know, I suppose so, but I had my work to think of, hadn't I?' He paused, his brows creased in an effort to recall the past and to present it in a not too damaging light. 'During the few months from the time we met until we parted in Torquay it was as though I was permanently drunk. I mean, here was I, an ordinary chap to whom this tremendous thing had happened! That's how it seemed to me at the time – you understand?' He was pathetically anxious to be understood, like most people with a guilty conscience. '*Nothing* else mattered. If she'd been married to my own brother it wouldn't have made any difference.'

'And yet you walked out on her.'

The young couple were back on their boat. She was lying face downwards on the cabin roof, she had removed her bra and he was rubbing her back with sun lotion. Byrne was watching them, his mind in a whirl. He had rationalized and tidied up the whole episode with Julie months ago, before he got married, seeing himself, relatively, in a favourable light. At least he had had the sense to get away from a dangerous woman! Now here was this grave-faced policeman turning the whole thing topsy turvy, making it seem that he had been the prime mover, that he was in the girl's debt, that he had 'walked out on her'!

'Why did you leave her?'

He clasped his hands round one knee and rocked gently to and fro in his chair. 'I suppose I realized that there was no future in it.' It was not the answer he would have given ten minutes earlier.

'You came back together?'

'No, I left her in Torquay, I didn't even know that she had come back until I heard that she was appearing at the club.'

'Did you see her again?'

'No. About a year ago I heard that she had left the town. I got married shortly afterwards and I neither saw nor heard anything of her until last week.'

'Then?'

'I had a letter from her saying that she was coming back and that she might look me up for old times' sake.'

'You still have the letter?'

'No, I destroyed it in case Gwyn should come across it.'

'Did she tell you where to find her?'

'No.'

'Did you try to find her?'

He shook his head. 'No, I was terrified that she would come looking for me.'

'You didn't go to the Marina?'

'I swear I didn't. I might have done if I'd known, just to persuade her to let bygones be bygones.'

Wycliffe sat back in his chair. 'All right, Mr Byrne, thank you for coming, I'll get in touch if I need you again.'

'You'll remember about Gwyn – not knowing?' The eyes were pleading.

'I'll remember.' He almost added, 'Why don't you tell her before her friends do?' But his job was crime not marriage guidance. All the same he chuckled as he went in to his lonely lunch. 'I wonder if he's managed to teach Gwyn any of Julie's little tricks.'

He had just finished his lunch and was considering smoking a pipe on the terrace when he was paged by the loudspeakers. Fehling was on the telephone, obviously pleased with himself.

'Any luck?'

'Kathy Johnson identified Masson-Smythe as the man she found going through the register at the Marina. I found out that he patronizes the bar at the Royal on Sunday mornings so I sent DC Hartley along with Kathy to have a drink. She's positive he's the man.'

'Good!'

'And we've picked up Pellow. He was a bit truculent at first but once he realized we had it on him he was ready to cough fast enough. Actually he's not too sorry to get one in on the Masson-Smythes for getting mixed up with Allen. "A small time runt who'd grass on his own mother!" – Pellow's description.'

Wycliffe could almost sympathize. No professional would have loused up an organization like the Voodoo, if only because he might need it one day.

'He's admitted to three other cases in the past eighteen months, including Frank Ellison.'

'The Hatton Garden chap?'

'That's the man. Eighty thousand pounds' worth of uncut stones, never traced.'

'It will be a feather in your cap if you can get a line on that lot, Mr Fehling!' But to tell the truth, Wycliffe was not interested. 'Where is Pellow now?'

'In the cells.'

'And Allen?'

'We packed him off on the train this morning.'

'No news of Jim Gill yet?'

'He only arrived in London at six this morning, sir.'

'All right. You've done very well, Mr Fehling. Did you get any sleep last night?'

'A few hours, sir.'

'What about lunch?'

'I've had a canteen lunch, sir, but don't worry about me, if there's anything I can do . . . '

Fehling had the enthusiasm of a very young schoolboy. Wycliffe hesitated. 'I'll ring you back in a few minutes.' He dropped the receiver, looked up the number of the Voodoo and dialled.

'Masson-Smythe speaking.'

'Chief Superintendent Wycliffe.'

'Yes?' A blend of caution and habitual self confidence.

'I would like to see you as soon as possible.'

Thelma's voice in the background: 'Who is it?' And her husband too concerned to remember to cover the mouthpiece: 'Wycliffe.'

'Shall we say this afternoon at the police station?'

A momentary hesitation. 'I'm afraid that this afternoon will not be convenient, perhaps tomorrow at my office.'

Wycliffe recognized the professional, feeling out the ground. He was decisive. 'I think that it had better be this afternoon, here.'

'Very well, if you insist, though what more I can tell you . . . '

'Let us say at two thirty, then.'

A moment later Wycliffe was speaking to Fehling again. 'I've made an appointment with Masson-Smythe at the station for two thirty and I want you to keep it. Question him about his travel agency – lean on him, but keep off the girl and her death. I'll give you an hour, then I'll take over.'

Fehling was pleased.

The superintendent spent half an hour on the terrace. He then strolled through the deserted streets to the police station. It seemed that most of the population must be on the beach or out in boats and the square had been taken over by the pigeons, strutting up and down between the rows of parked cars. Outside the station, an E-type Jag, parked against the kerb. The wages of sin. From the desk he phoned Fehling, who came down a few minutes later.

'We've got him, sir. He's a slippery customer but he knows that he can't talk his way out of this one. We can slap half a dozen charges on him over the Allen business but it's going to be the devil of a job to get him on the others. It's Pellow's word against his.'

Wycliffe looked sympathetic but at heart he was only interested in Masson-Smythe in so far as he might shed light on Julie's murder. 'All right, I'll take over now and you can have another go later.'

Masson-Smythe was in Wycliffe's office, sitting in the chair by the desk. He looked changed; despite his natty summer suiting in fashionable cinnamon, he looked bedraggled. He was holding his glasses in his hand, leaving white circles round his eyes in contrast with his flushed features.

'Well, Mr Smythe, this man Allen seems to have caused both of us quite a lot of trouble.'

Masson-Smythe looked at him dully. Wycliffe beamed. 'Amateurs! Fortunately you and I are professionals and we know the score.'

Masson-Smythe said nothing but wiped his glasses and put them back on.

Wycliffe turned over the papers on his desk. 'You told me that you employed Julie Collins in your cabaret on the strength of a visit she made to your club on a rehearsal afternoon. You auditioned her and offered her a four month contract.'

'That is correct.'

'You did not tell me that for some time before you had, as the phrase goes, been on terms of intimacy with her.'

Masson-Smythe drew out a silver cigarette case. 'May I smoke?' He lit a Turkish cigarette and blew a cloud of pungent, silver grey smoke into the air. He was recovering confidence. 'I answered the questions you asked, superintendent.'

'I see. Would it be true to say, then, that you engaged her because she threatened to tell your wife of your relationship?'

'That would not be true. I offered her a contract because I thought she had the makings of a first-class cabaret artiste and events have proved me right.'

Wycliffe smiled. 'A club like yours, although it makes its money out of visitors, depends for its continued existence on the good will or at least the tolerance of influential locals. Knowing this, you employ the wife of one of the town's most respected business men simply because she's pretty good at taking her clothes off in public. Frankly, I don't believe it!' He brought out his half-smoked pipe and relit it, watching Masson-Smythe over the undulant flame of the match. 'But that is unimportant . . . ' He broke off abruptly, looking across at DC Rees who sat in the corner taking notes. 'I suppose Mr Masson-Smythe has been formally cautioned? . . . Good! We must keep the record straight.'

The superintendent seemed to be in no hurry, he shuffled through the litter of papers on his desk and then, without looking up, 'What were you doing in the Marina on Monday evening?' Make your man comfortable, then kick the chair away.

Masson-Smythe stopped with his cigarette halfway to his lips. 'I don't know what you're talking about.'

Wycliffe was as bland as mother's milk. 'Oh, come, Mr Smythe! I have a statement here from a witness; not a shadow of doubt. In any case I can't see why you need be so coy. After all, we know that it was at Julie's instigation that you were arranging Allen's passage. Surely, that's what you've been talking to Mr Fehling about?'

Masson-Smythe leaned forward in his chair. 'All right, I went to the Marina to see her but she wasn't in.'

'So when did you see her?'

Now he was like a chess player, trying to foresee his opponent's next move. His hand went to his waistcoat pocket and his fingers searched for something they did not find. 'She telephoned me.'

'Saying what?' Wycliffe was intrigued by the movement of his right hand, he was passing his thumb over his fingers continuously in a rolling movement. A nervous idiosyncrasy, but an odd one.

'She telephoned to fix up details about Allen.'

'She must have had a considerable hold over you for you to take on that job. After all, Allen hadn't a penny and you must have known that he was no more than a petty thief. She was blackmailing you, wasn't she, Mr Smythe?'

Again the fruitless investigation of his waistcoat pocket and a resumption of the rolling movement of fingers and thumb.

'Think about your answer by all means. I have a colleague in London at this moment, searching her flat. I also have a witness who will state that Julie had a hold over both you and your wife while she was still under contract at the club. You were in a cleft stick over this man Allen. Far from turning him down or even making a little on the deal, you had to subsidize him. Julie had a thousand pounds in notes in her room when she died – when did you hand them over, Mr Smythe?'

'I gave her no money, I swear it!' Fingers and thumb were working overtime now, and suddenly their message was clear to Wycliffe. He put his hand into the pocket of his jacket and his fingers closed over a little steel ball-bearing, the one Fehling had found under the girl's bed.

'Do you think we could have the window open?' Masson-Smythe was sweating profusely, the perspiration running down his temples and filming his spectacles.

Wycliffe got up and opened the window himself, letting in the raucous screaming of gulls who were quarrelling over scraps thrown out from the canteen.

'I don't deny that I have given her money in the past. If your people have searched her flat they must have evidence that she was blackmailing me anyway.'

'How much and how often?'

'Perhaps five or six hundred over the past year.'

'Not bleeding you, then?'

'No, I had the impression that she thought I might be useful in other ways and, of course, I was right.'

'Her threat was exposure to the police?'

'She didn't threaten.' He lit another cigarette and inhaled deeply. He was silent for some time and Wycliffe let him be. The little clock on the mantelpiece dominated the room with its loud metallic tick. When he next spoke his whole manner seemed to have changed. 'I've knocked about the world since I was a boy of sixteen and there isn't much that can surprise me now. But that girl . . . ! I knew I was a damn fool to get mixed up with her. She was a shrewd, calculating bitch, but she had what it takes to hold a man. She was like a drug, you kept coming back though you knew she would finish you in the end. I was like a kid with his first girl.'

'How did she find out?'

He laughed. 'Pillow talk! Me! I wanted to impress her and she would lie there with her ears pinned back cooing away and then – Wham!' The suave tight-lipped mask had slipped to reveal a coarser, more violent personality underneath. His speech was different, even his postural reflexes seemed to have changed for he lounged in his chair where previously he had sat almost primly, conscious of his dignity. Now he looked out of place in his smart dandified clothes.

But he had stopped the rolling movement of his fingers and thumb, the tension had gone.

Wycliffe looked at the almost expressionless, almost immobile features and suddenly he understood. 'It was something more than your little racket which Julie held over you, wasn't it? It was not so much what you were doing as *who you were*.'

'There's no point in denying it now, is there, copper? I've known for eight years that I had only to get myself nicked once and it would be all up.' He stroked his cheek. 'They can alter your face but they can't change your dabs.'

'Where did you break from?'

'The Moor.'

It had become a parlour guessing game with Smythe furnishing the clues and Wycliffe doing the guessing.

'Eight years ago . . . McClaren, the bank robber.' Wycliffe racked his memory. 'A bank in Holborn, you and three others, a bystander was shot and killed – shot when he tried to interfere. You got over the wall with . . . '

'Nick Crane but he was picked up.' Masson-Smythe seemed delighted to be remembered as though they were old friends meeting after a lapse of years.

Wycliffe remembered the case, not because he was involved, but because of the cold-blooded killing of a courageous young man who had tried to stop them getting away. 'You got fifteen years and you served two . . . '

'Three.'

'And they never recovered the money.'

'No.'

Young Rees had become so absorbed in the drama being played out before him that he had forgotten to take notes. Not that it mattered, Masson-Smythe, or McClaren, had gone beyond the point of no return. Wycliffe picked up the telephone. 'Ask Dr Rashleigh if he will kindly come to the station to do a blood test – a grouping test . . . Yes, as soon as possible, please.'

'What's that in aid of?'

'You'll see.'

'I didn't kill her.'

'No? You had ample motive and you've killed before.'

'That's not true. I didn't know there was a shooter in the outfit. Even the judge said there was no evidence to show which of us fired the shot.'

He was right, the gun had been left at the scene and it hadn't been possible to establish which of the three men had used it.

'Why did you go to the Marina on Tuesday night?'

'You mean Monday, surely?'

'Don't stall! It will do you no good as well you know! Why did you go to the girl on Tuesday night, the night she was killed?'

Smythe still hesitated and Wycliffe took the little steel ball from his pocket and lobbed it over. 'You left your calling card and you left the money – a thousand pounds in used notes.'

Smythe caught the steel ball, glanced at it and laid it on the desk in the ashtray. 'All right, I went there, but I didn't leave her any money.'

'Why did you go?'

'She insisted. As far as the money goes you can check my bank account . . . '

'A fat lot of good that would be. It would surprise me if you don't keep that amount of cash on hand. Anyway, if she didn't want money why did she tell you to come?'

He shook his head. 'I don't know but it was just like her. She could never resist cracking the whip. The point is, when I got there she was already dead.'

Wycliffe looked at him through narrowed eyes. 'You expect me to believe that?'

'It's straight up.'

'What time did you get there?'

'One o'clock was the time she gave me but I was early, say twenty or a quarter to.' He stopped to light a cigarette. 'The front door was unlocked as she told me it would be and I followed her directions. The bedroom door was a bit open and there was a light on. I think I called her name, but there was no answer and then I pushed the door wide open and went in . . . '

'Go on.'

'She was lying on the bed, naked. At first I thought that she was up to her games, then I thought she might be asleep and I touched her. She was warm but completely limp. I wondered if she was drugged but when I tried her heart and pulse there was nothing – not a dicky bird.'

'So?'

'I scarpered. I got out of that place like a bat out of hell! I mean, what else could I do?'

'When you saw her on the bed how did she look?'

'Look? I've just told you, like she was sleeping though it seemed a bit odd to be sleeping naked with no bedclothes over her.'

'Did you see a door-stop in the room? A brass weight?'

'Was that what it was? I nearly tripped over the bloody thing in the middle of the floor.'

'Did you have intercourse with her?'

'Christ, no! What sort of bloody pervert do you take me for?'

'Did you search her room?'

Masson-Smythe leaned forward in his chair. 'Look, skip, do me a favour and get this straight: I went to the room, I found her lying there, I made sure she was dead and I scarpered. With my problems what else could I do?' He looked at Wycliffe intently, his eyes anxious. 'You do believe me?'

'There's no reason why I should.' Wycliffe picked up the telephone once more. 'I'm having you taken down. Later you'll be asked to make a formal statement.'

DC Rees went out with Masson-Smythe and Wycliffe remained in his chair, staring into space. Was Smythe telling the truth? Convicted of robbery with violence, an escaped convict with the strongest motive for killing the girl, was it likely that someone else had murdered her and that he had arrived, innocently, to find her dead? Yet it was too easy to pin the thing on him. And what about the disfigurement? If Masson-Smythe had found her dead, did he then set about destroying her features? And if so, why? A sudden flooding tide of anger? Most professionals were not like that, they seldom let their hearts rule their heads. But had he a motive for disfiguring her? Perhaps. An unidentified corpse found in a hotel bedroom doesn't worry anybody much but the police *as long as it remains unidentified*. But Julie Collins's corpse would soon bring the cops to his doorstep.

Wycliffe sighed and turned his thoughts to Julie herself. He knew quite a lot about her now, but the facts, put together, made a strange pattern – or no pattern at all. Although he knew well enough that human motives are always complex, that every man is a battleground of conflicting desires and emotions, he had still found it useful to try to pin-point a single dominant drive in accounting for any course of action. Greed, jealousy, love, ambition, lust . . . Single words, powerful words, and convenient shorthand with which to label the motives of a man – or of a woman. But Julie refused to be pigeon-holed. His mental vision of her remained as enigmatic as his first actual sight of her, lying across her hotel bed, naked, in the posture of love.

Plenty of amateur psychologists would have little difficulty in explaining Julie. A neglected child, orphaned at an age when she needed a sense of security most – they would see in her ruthlessness, in the exercise of her power over men, a desire to hit back. And into her frenzied promiscuity they might read a continuing and unsatisfied yearning to identify herself with other human beings, to be accepted. Perhaps they would be right, but Wycliffe felt that such explanations were too facile, they were little better than his word labels. For one thing, neither Julie nor anyone else is simply a product of an environment. Nature, in his book, was at least as important as nurture. Look at Kathy Johnson. He got up from his chair, profoundly dissatisfied, and went into the HQ room.

It was empty but he could hear voices in the little office used by Fehling and Gill. He pushed open the door. Fehling heaved himself out of the chair behind the desk. 'Mr and Mrs Little, sir. Julie's foster parents.'

The Littles were in their late fifties. He was tall, his best suit hung loose on his bony frame and his face was creased with deep lines from nostrils to mouth. His domed head was bald and shining. A Geordie, he turned out to be, who had come south in the Depression and never gone back. His wife was local, plump, comfortable, with a mind of her own though ready enough to play second fiddle in deference to her belief in proper male dominance. They sat close, posed as though waiting for a picture to be taken.

'I only saw her photo in the paper after dinner when I settled down to have a read. It knocked us sideways and we thought we'd better come straight away . . . '

Mrs Little dabbed her eyes with a screwed-up handkerchief. 'I was telling this gentleman, nine years we had her, she was like our own flesh and blood.'

Under some pressure they admitted that Julie had not been an easy child. 'But we loved her none the less for that!' Mrs Little's features threatened to dissolve at any moment into uncontrollable weeping. 'Once we thought they might make us take her away from school.' She lowered her voice and murmured the dreaded word – 'Stealing! And no need for it, we'd always given her everything she wanted, hadn't we, Bert?'

Mr Little nodded and blinked. He had a habit of blinking nervously whenever he was addressed. 'And we had a bit of trouble with boys – not that I'm narrow, we didn't mind her having boy friends, but this was different. She got herself mixed up with a lot of young thugs. The things we found in her room! I mean it was obvious that she was going all the way and her not fifteen!' He broke off and sighed. 'But she was reasonable, she listened, which is more than some of them will.' He blinked furiously.

'And she was such a clever girl!' Mrs Little redressed the balance. 'You should see her school reports – everything "Excellent" – all her subjects, only at the bottom her headmaster would write something about her attitude and conduct being unsatisfactory.'

'What about her marriage?'

They looked at each other and tacitly agreed that it was mother's turn. 'We didn't know anything about it until young Collins came along and asked our permission. We was taken aback, I can tell you! At first we was all against it; for one thing she was too young to marry and he was a man of thirty-six . . . '

Mr Little, revolving his trilby hat in his lap, took up the tale: 'Of course it wasn't for us to decide really, it was up to the Children's Officer, but we talked it over and in the end we agreed it might be the best thing for her. She was set on it anyway.'

'It was a good chance,' Mrs Little said. 'The Collinses are a respected family in the town, she wouldn't want for anything. But it didn't work.'

'Have you heard from her since she went away?'

Mrs Little shook her head and her husband answered, 'Not so much as a Christmas card.'

'Did you know her parents?'

Mrs Little looked at her husband, her tiny mouth pursed in disapproval. He blinked and said, 'Yes, we knew them.'

'We used to feel sorry for the little girl, they neglected her, always gallivanting off and leaving her to fend for herself, poor little mite!'

'Her mother was on the stage before she married him – or said she was. She made up enough.'

'He was a carpenter, wasn't he?' Wycliffe asked.

Mr Little smiled. 'You could call him that, I suppose. He used to make old-fashioned chairs and tables in a shed behind the house. I suppose he must have sold them because they never seemed to be short of money.'

'He was all right in his way,' Mrs Little argued. 'It was her!'

'They lived near you?'

'Next door when we lived down on the Plain, before we moved to the estate. Julie used to spend most of her time in our place even then.'

CHAPTER ELEVEN

It was after eight when Gill finally telephoned and Wycliffe had been sitting at his desk since six. From time to time he pretended to work on the reports but most of the time he dozed. His head would sag on his chest and he was asleep. It was a warm evening and he envied the people still messing about in boats in the harbour, the sea like glass on the evening flood. He even envied the people in church with the west doors open and the sun streaming down the nave. When the phone rang he woke with a start and it took him a moment to remember where he was. 'Any luck?'

'Not so's you'd notice. It's no rest cure trying to find anybody in London on a fine Sunday. Anyway I had a word with the owner of the strip joints where she used to work and with her landlady of those days. Nothing much we don't know already. Then I ran down the manager of the night club where she's under contract – or was. I found him at a sort of pansies' *soirée* in Camden Town. He was a mite peeved at first . . . '

'Never mind the local colour, let's have the facts,' Wycliffe growled.

'Yes, sir! He's definitely cheesed off. Says he'll lose a mint through this. Apparently her act was a sensation. She used to come on all in white silk, down to her ankles, hair to her shoulders, innocent and virginal. Then she'd sing obscene little ditties in a husky contralto. All the time she'd never fetch a smile and look vaguely shocked when the audience laughed their heads off. The manager told me she's already made two records and was all set to be a money spinner.'

'There are easier ways of making a living than being a policeman.'

Gill cackled. 'You can say that again. You ought to see this chick's bankbook! Lovely figures all down one side – in black.'

'I gather you've been to her flat?'

'Eager Beaver – that's me! Nice place, nice neighbourhood. People don't care what you do as long as you don't disturb them doing it. Her place, all white and oatmeal . . . '

'What? I thought you said oatmeal?'

'I did, it's a sort of beige . . . '

'Never mind. Any books?'

'Books? Hundreds! Place is like a public library. Some of them are quite interesting.'

'In what way?'

'Let's call them text books of sexual technology. She must have made a study of it.'

'I expect she did, it was her living one way or another.'

'She seems to have done a spot of blackmail as a sideline – nothing spectacular – chicken feed compared with what she got more or less legit. A little book with several addresses and against one or two of them sums of money at intervals. Amounts between fifty and three or four hundred. One of the providers is on our patch – our friend Masson-Smythe.'

'I've been talking to him this afternoon. Any evidence?'

'Evidence?'

'Don't be difficult, Jim! If she's blackmailing she must have something.'

'Not a thing!'

That was the irony of it. So many victims of blackmail

are paying up on evidence long since destroyed.

'Anything else?'

'No, sir. Sufficient unto the day . . .'

'You'd better come home, my lad.'

Wycliffe put the telephone back on its rest, stretched and yawned. Sufficient unto the day . . . It was too late for dinner but he would be able to get cold meat and salad.

He had his cold meat and salad with half a bottle of Beaujolais, but only just. He was sitting back and thinking about lighting his pipe when the loudspeaker paged him. Helen, her hair bleached, her skin pink after a day on the water, looked at him with concern. 'You're dog tired.'

'Don't be silly, I've been sleeping most of the evening!'

It was Fehling, who had been given the job of getting a warrant and organizing the search of the Voodoo premises. 'I was beginning to think that every magistrate had emigrated! Anyway, I made it in the end. I'm speaking from the club now.'

'Any luck?'

Fehling was hesitant. 'Of course we're not through yet, sir, but I've got a feeling this place is clean. There's nothing here which could incriminate a monk. They were ready for us!'

Wycliffe was not very interested but he tried to sound consoling. 'I shouldn't worry, we've got more than enough to cook Masson-Smythe's goose.'

'That's not the point, sir! I was counting on getting a lead on some of his pals – past and present.'

'Very frustrating!' Wycliffe couldn't get worked up over Fehling's yearning for promotion. 'Anything else?'

'Yes, the Masson-Smythe woman made a break for it just before I arrived. Not very clever! Apparently she phoned for a taxi and when it arrived just turned up on the step all ready for the off. Of course, DC Hartley, who was keeping obo, put paid to that! He's with me now, by the way, not much point in him going back on obo when . . . '

'None,' Wycliffe agreed. He saw no reason so far for stirring out of the hotel again. He wished that Fehling would dry up and he struggled to light his pipe with the receiver wedged between his cheek and his shoulder.

'There was one other thing, sir. In a drawer of Smythe's desk I found a silver framed photograph of the dead girl. I wondered . . . '

'The one from her dressing table?' Wycliffe was on the ball now. All that kerfuffle before coming to the point! Of course it might not *be* the point for Fehling.

'It could be, sir. We shall have to show it to the girl at the Marina.'

'Prints?'

'Only one or two smears, nothing identifiable.'

'I'll be down. Give me ten minutes.'

Thelma Masson-Smythe was composed and inclined to offence rather than defence. 'I don't know by what right . . . '

Wycliffe ignored her. She was lounging among the cushions of an overblown settee like some Hollywood *femme fatale* of the twenties. Her baggage, two suitcases, was still on the floor beside her.

'Open them up,' to Hartley who hovered in the background.

'They've been searched, sir, there's nothing . . . '

'Never mind, open them.'

Hartley lifted one of the cases on to a chair, snapped the catches and lifted the lid. Thelma Masson-Smythe sat up to get a better view. Her manner was indifferent, almost sardonic. The case was half empty, a few underclothes thrown in on two or three summer dresses neatly folded in polythene bags. Wycliffe lifted out a couple of slips, a brassiere and two pairs of briefs.

'You get a kick out of that?' As with her husband, the thin veneer was peeling off and the real woman beginning to show through, a hard-faced tart.

The second case held a coat and skirt, a nightdress and a few more items of underwear. Wycliffe closed the lid and turned to the woman. He was puzzled; sure that she had hoaxed them, but he could not see what she had achieved by doing it. 'You intended to travel light?' The first words he had spoken to her since his arrival.

She puffed cigarette smoke ceilingwards and watched it rise. 'I was in a hurry.' The plain orange dress she wore was sleeveless, tight, and so brief that it made Wycliffe slightly uneasy to look at her, embarrassed by the sheer bulk of naked pink flesh.

'No woman is in too much of a hurry to put in her toilet things.'

'I forgot.'

Wycliffe lit his pipe. 'You were told this afternoon that your husband had been arrested and that you would be able to talk to him if you came to the station.'

'I'm not responsible for his troubles!'

Wycliffe left her, still puzzled and disgruntled, and wandered about the premises, watching Fehling's men at work, searching every drawer, every cupboard. No stone unturned. But he agreed with the inspector, it was a waste of time. He looked at the silver framed photograph of the dead girl, a head and shoulders, a colour print like the stills outside cinemas.

'You think Masson-Smythe took it when he went to the Marina?' Fehling asked.

'It's possible.'

Fehling shook his massive head. 'I don't see why he should have unless he also battered her face in. I mean, if he wanted to destroy clues to her identity, there wouldn't be much point in taking the photo and leaving the girl . . . '

They were in Smythe's office and Wycliffe perched himself on the edge of the desk. 'Have you thought that it might have been a woman who did the battering?'

It was obvious that the idea had not occurred to Fehling, equally obvious that he was taken by it. 'Thelma?'

'I don't know.'

'She could have followed her husband . . . ' He was getting enthusiastic. 'By all accounts she had reason enough to hate the girl.'

Wycliffe was still holding the photograph and he began to remove it from its frame. 'There, on the back in pencil: *Voodoo* and a serial number. That would be reason enough for Smythe to take it away with him, it was one of his publicity shots of the girl and he wouldn't want that found beside her body . . . '

'The same would apply to Thelma.'

'Of course!' He was chasing an elusive idea which had nothing to do with the photograph. 'Why did she call a taxi?'

Fehling looked surprised. 'To make a bolt for it, I suppose.'

'Nonsense! She's too wily a bird not to know that we had the place covered.'

'Then I don't follow . . . '

'She *wanted* to be stopped. She had no intention of taking that taxi.' He broke off. 'Send for Hartley.'

DC Hartley was a Wiltshireman and his voice would have been God's gift to a radio gardening programme. 'Sir?'

'Did anybody enter the premises during the evening before Mrs Masson-Smythe tried to leave?'

Hartley's expression was sufficient answer.

'All right, you forgot, what happened afterwards put it out of your mind . . . '

'I noted it, sir.' He brought out his notebook and flipped over the pages. 'Four thirty, sir. A girl, blonde, smallish, light blue summer dress and white handbag. . . '

'When did she come out?'

Hartley flushed. 'She didn't, sir.'

'Then she must be here now. Have you found her?' Nasty. Wycliffe didn't wait for a reply but turned to Fehling. 'That's where your evidence is gone. Now, Hartley, what did you do when you saw Mrs Masson-Smythe about to clear out in a taxi?'

'I went over and stopped her, sir.'

'Was she abusive?'

'Resigned, I would have said, sir. She didn't seem very surprised.'

'What did you do then?'

'Why, I went in with her to the lounge, I was about to phone through to the station and report when Inspector Fehling turned up . . . '

'And while you were escorting her indoors, the other young woman skipped out with a suitcase containing what Inspector Fehling is looking for.'

'And now,' said Fehling, ominously, 'we're looking for a smallish blonde who wears a light blue dress and carries a white handbag. Hartley!'

Wycliffe had found that the chance to play the great detective came rarely and when it did you had to avoid sounding smug. 'I should try 4a, Mount Zion, Hartley. Ask for Sadie Field.'

'The stripper?' Fehling was incredulous. 'I thought you said she was a decent sort of girl?'

'She is but she's also a bit dumb and scared of losing her job, just the sort Thelma would choose to do her dirty work. In any case, Sadie won't have heard yet that her employer has been nicked.'

'Well! What are you waiting for, Hartley?' Fehling was smarting a bit.

'Go easy on her!' Wycliffe ordered. 'She's more sinned against than sinning.'

He wandered out of the office and down the steps to the club. The lights were on, and two solemn dicks were shaking one of the giant polystyrene statues between them, to see if it rattled. It was too much for Wycliffe and he made his way back to the lounge.

Thelma seemed not to have moved but she was sipping a drink and there was a tray of drinks on a small table by the settee. 'Found what you're looking for, superintendent? If you would tell me what it is, perhaps I could help you?'

Wycliffe perched on the arm of a voluptuous black leather monster which seemed ready to engulf and perhaps digest anyone with the temerity to sit in it properly.

'Whisky, superintendent?' Her assurance was brittle and when he merely sat and stared at her without speaking he was gratified to see her shift her position slightly and make an ineffective effort to pull down the hem of her dress.

'I found an interesting photograph, a photograph of Julie Collins in a silver frame. It was last seen on the dressing table in her bedroom at the Marina.'

She stopped with her glass midway to her lips. 'That's not possible.'

'Oh, it's possible all right, your husband admits that he went to see the girl on the night she was murdered. He says, of course, that she was dead when he got there.'

She was off the settee in a flash, upsetting her drink down the front of her dress. 'You filthy, lying, stinking cop! You can't pin that on him!'

Wycliffe was unmoved. 'That remains to be seen, but what interests me at the moment is your share in the business.'

'Me?' Her surprise could have been genuine. Standing there with the gin soaking into the bodice of her dress, without shoes, her hair and eyes wild, it was hard to connect her with the woman in the blue gown whom Helen had described as 'striking', who moved about the club, suave and graceful, the experienced professional hostess.

'You haven't been told that Julie's face was destroyed by an attacker who battered her with a heavy brass weight.'

This stopped her. She went to the settee and sat on the edge, her legs apart, her hands drooping between them. 'Serves her bloody well right, she was a dirty whore!'

'You had reason to be jealous of her. Is it possible that you followed your husband that night . . . ?'

'Me? You think that I . . . ?'

'You hated the girl and you are obviously vicious.'

'You can't set me up, copper!' But there was no longer any punch behind the words. She was shaken, and she continued to sit in the same posture as before, for once unselfconscious, like a little girl, a little girl with a problem.

He drove back to his hotel. The town was deserted and as he passed through the square the town clock was doling out the strokes of midnight. The hotel garage was full so he left his car in the forecourt. The night porter admitted him. 'Developments, sir?' Wycliffe grunted. He had his foot on the carpeted stair, then he noticed that there was still light in the television lounge.

'They're down, sir.'

'Down?'

'The astronauts, they've touched down on the moon.'

He had forgotten and the fact unsettled him. But he did not go into the television lounge, instead he went through to the terrace. He lit his pipe and rested his arms on the balustrade, staring out over the harbour. It was very quiet, a noise of purring machinery from the docks, and that was all. He could make out the shape of the little sailing boat belonging to the young couple. There was a riding light at the masthead and he thought that he could distinguish a dim glow from the porthole of the tiny cabin.

Tonight men would walk on the moon. He tried to take it in, to grasp and hold the thought that this moment of time was shared with two men in their fragile capsule on the surface of the moon a quarter of a million miles away. He tried and failed. It was when he made an effort to think in a disciplined way about anything that he was most conscious of his shortcomings. And this reflection brought him back to the case. Not only did he find sustained logical thought difficult but he was always short of written data. He had the official reports but these were so full as to be almost useless. Any other detective would have a sheaf of private notes, but he rarely wrote anything down and if he did he either lost it or threw it away. Notes were repugnant to him. Even now he ought to be sitting at a desk with a notepad in front of him, jotting down his ideas, transposing and relating facts like a jig-saw.

Like hell!

But the price he paid was heavy, his thoughts went in circles.

Julie Collins had been strangled, then viciously assaulted. If Masson-Smythe spoke the truth, one did not immediately follow the other. Had the murderer been interrupted in his work? Had he retreated somewhere when he heard Smythe coming? The figure on the fire-escape? It seemed improbable. He could only have left the girl's room through the door, in which case Smythe would almost certainly have seen him. *Had* Smythe seen him? Unlikely but not impossible. But if the murderer had already gone when Masson-Smythe arrived, that presupposed that someone else had come after him and disfigured the girl.

Had the man on the fire-escape watched the murder, seen Smythe enter and leave, and *then* come in through the bathroom window to carry out his task? But why?

There was movement on the little yacht, a lithe figure climbing on to the cabin roof, standing by the mast; the glimmer of a cigarette.

And if Smythe was lying? It was possible though unlikely that the man who had intercourse with the girl was not her murderer. That let Smythe out, for according to Rashleigh he was Group O. But he could have been responsible for the disfigurement to make identification difficult and reduce the risk of being linked with the crime. Far fetched? But there had to be some explanation and if he had rejected every far fetched hypothesis in his cases a good many would have remained unsolved.

The girl had joined her lover, they were standing side by side now, he could see the glow of both cigarettes; from time to time one or the other would describe a small trajectory in the darkness.

As to suspects, he had plenty. Allen, Smythe, Collins, Byrne – though he could hardly take Byrne seriously. And if hate was the motive for the mutilation, who had better reason to hate her than the women?

He went inside.

'Not staying up for the walk, sir?'

'No.'

As he slid in beside his wife he could feel the glowing warmth from her sun-tanned skin. 'You'll be sore tomorrow,' he whispered.

CHAPTER TWELVE

He woke with his course of action clear in his mind and with the confidence that it would bring results. By the time he went to bed again the case would be over. A sanguine view considering his vague speculations of the previous night but it was a familiar pattern. Somehow the alchemy of sleep had once more cleared and ordered his thoughts. He could not explain it, he just knew, and because he knew he hummed a little tune in the bathroom. Helen, still in bed, called to him, 'You sound happy this morning!'

'I am! How are the shoulders?'

'Sore.'

'That'll teach you to go to sea decently clad.'

'The twins rang up last night.' The Wycliffes had twin children, a boy and a girl of nineteen and they had been camping in France.

'Oh, they're back are they?'

'They came back on somebody's yacht of all things – somebody they met in Cherbourg while they were waiting for the ferry.'

He couldn't help remembering his own youth when a day trip to Barmouth was something to look forward to and back on for weeks.

He was in the bedroom now, in his dressing gown. Out of the window he could see the little boat belonging to the young couple. They were swimming again, although it was raining. For some reason he felt a sudden pang of sadness and sighed.

'What's the matter?'

'Old age – what else?'

Before breakfast they watched a telerecording of the moon walk. 'That's one small step for man, one giant leap for mankind.' Neil Armstrong's words, they impressed him. He wondered why he felt that men who walked on the moon should have come from a better world.

When he arrived at the station there were half-a-dozen pressmen lounging round the enquiry desk, including Brown from the local paper.

'Good morning, lads!'

'Has Masson-Smythe been arrested?'

'What's he charged with?'

'Off the record . . . '

'Is the case over?'

Wycliffe lit his pipe. 'If you got all the answers you know very well you couldn't print 'em. Mr Masson-Smythe was with me yesterday afternoon . . . '

' . . . helping with enquiries!' they finished for him.

'Exactly! However, certain charges have been made but they have no direct connection with the murder.'

'What are the charges?'

'He will be coming up before the magistrates this morning.'

'What about Allen?'

'He is back in custody and, presumably, the law will proceed against him where it left off.'

'But he slugged you on Friday night at the club.'

'Did he? I shouldn't print that if I were you, he might have you for libel.'

One shrivelled little fellow who looked in need of a good meal but was, in fact, the most experienced of them, spoke for the first time. 'The super promised a statement and that's all we're going to get. Let's have it.'

'Good! Here it is: "For reasons connected with the

inquiry, the police have not previously disclosed that the dead girl's features had been so mutilated after death as to make them unrecognizable." '

This silenced them and by the time they found fresh questions Wycliffe was half-way up the stairs to his office. Fehling was waiting for him. 'What about the Spaniard? He's due to sail at six this evening.'

'Let him!' Wycliffe growled. 'We've got enough crooks of our own.'

It was half past nine when he arrived at the bookshop. The little rat-faced man was scrubbing the steps but Wycliffe went to the side door. He did not ring, it was unlocked, so he climbed the carpeted stairs without invitation. At the top he called, 'Is anyone at home?' Aunt Jane came out of the kitchen at the end of the dimly lit corridor.

'I'm extremely sorry! I hope you don't mind me coming up but I think your bell must be out of order.'

'Superintendent!' She was all of a flutter but welcoming. 'Let me get out of this overall. Just step into the lounge, superintendent, I'll be with you in a moment.'

He found himself once more in the depressing room overlooking the street; nothing had changed. He stood by the window watching the traffic until she joined him. She was nervous, alternately patting her cropped hair and smoothing the creases from her blue linen dress. Except for a difference in length, it seemed to be a replica of a dress Wycliffe's grandmother had worn when he first remembered her. She made him sit down in one of the easy chairs and perched herself on one of the straightbacks.

'I'm glad to see you recovered, Miss Collins.'

'Oh, yes, I'm quite recovered, thank you, superintendent. They wanted me to spend a few days in a nursing home but I told them I have a few things to clear up here first. After that we shall see.'

Wycliffe scarcely knew where to begin.

'By all means smoke, superintendent! My father and my brother smoked a pipe and I like the smell of tobacco.'

It was something. He lit up.

'It was clever of you to come, superintendent.'

'Clever?'

'Of course! To realize that it was I who could tell you about Willie. Ada is his mother but she's never been *close* to him. Even when he was a little boy it was to me that he came with all his troubles and we would sit down together and work something out. He was such a sensitive child, superintendent, and Ada never really understood him. Willie is a Collins.'

'You've lived here for a long time, Miss Collins?'

'All my life, it's my home.' She looked down at her large bony hands, clasped in her lap. 'Ada always frustrated Willie; she still does. She seems to think it's a sin for people to do what they want, a sin not to be always *busy*. Yet we know our Lord's answer to Martha, don't we?' She spoke as though they shared a cosy but rather guilty secret. 'I can remember so well, when Willie was a little boy, she used to say, "You can play with your soldiers, Willie, but only until tea-time", "You can read *one* chapter of your book", or "You can go out for half-an-hour". Of course, she was just the same with his father. I've always said he wouldn't have gone like he did if it hadn't been for her.'

'And Willie still comes to you with his troubles?'

She flashed him a quick, anxious look from her slightly protuberant eyes, and for some reason her lower lip trembled. He was afraid that she would cry but she recovered herself. 'He always confides in me.'

'Did he tell you that Julie had written to him to say that she was coming back?'

Her face hardened. 'Iris has been talking to you, I know. She's no right, she's only an employee!'

Wycliffe stood up. 'I could call him up and ask him now . . . '

'No!' Her reaction was so sharp that it startled him. 'No, I don't want him here.' She smoothed the material of her dress. 'He told me.'

'Did he think that she was coming back to him?'

'He hoped that she would.'

'And you?'

'I wanted what he wanted.'

He could see her mental conflict reflected in her face. 'She was a slut!' And she added, 'He would never have married her if it hadn't been for Ada's scheming.'

'When did you give him the money, Miss Collins?'

Her jaw set in a firm line. 'I don't know what you're talking about!'

He was gentle. 'I can get a court order in a case of this sort. Your bank would have to tell the truth.'

She gave in at once. 'Ada always kept him short! My brother never intended it to be like that. He left the business to Ada for her lifetime, just to protect her, but she's used the will to keep her son tied to her apron strings. The poor boy's never had any money of his own, just the pittance he draws as salary . . . It makes my blood boil!'

'So you gave him a thousand pounds in cash. What did he say it was for?'

'For Julie. He told me exactly what it was for, we don't have any secrets from each other. The money was for her.'

'Why, exactly, did she need a thousand pounds?'

'She said in her letter that she was in trouble with the

police and that she needed the money to avoid going to prison. She hinted that if he helped her she would come back to him.'

'You believed all this?'

She gave him an odd look. 'Certainly not! But he did. It was very thinly disguised blackmail!'

'Yet you let him go through with it – gave him the money to go through with it.'

She laughed without humour. 'You don't keep people's love by telling them the truth, superintendent. You have to let them find that out for themselves – then be there waiting for them.'

Love should never repel but Wycliffe was repelled. The Marina seemed to him at that moment a haven of sanity and decency compared with this little bourgeois household. But what was the point in making such comparisons? Such judgements? People lived their lives and who was he to moralize? He had never had the Collinses for a family or Julie for a wife. If he had, who could say?

She sat watching him, a tentative smile on her lips. 'Anyhow, it will come right now.'

'Come right?'

'She's dead, isn't she?'

'Murdered.'

She shook her head.

'Julie was strangled, Miss Collins, there can be no doubt of that.'

But she continued to shake her head.

'Are you afraid that it was Willie who killed her? Perhaps you know that it was he – did he confide in you?'

The look she gave him sprang from a sudden flare of hatred. 'Don't be absurd! Willie wouldn't hurt a fly, you have only to look at him . . . Nobody but a fool would . . . '

'Then what are you afraid of?'

'That you will get things wrong.' She made an effort to control herself. 'After all, you don't know him as I do.'

Wycliffe looked at her for some time, his eyes steady and grave. At last she raised hers and their gaze met. They sat for a little longer in silence, then Wycliffe stood up. 'Well, Miss Collins, thank you for talking to me. I will go through the bookroom, if I may, to the shop.'

'You are going to see him?'

'There are one or two points.'

She would have liked to stop him but she realized that she was helpless. 'Very well! You know the way. But remember, superintendent, he's not himself.'

He went down to the next landing while she stood at the top of the stairs watching. The only light in the corridor and down the stairs came from fanlights over the doors of the rooms. The atmosphere was oppressive, claustrophobic. He paused at the green baize door. 'To spend one's whole life in such a place!'

One old gentleman burrowed among the books but otherwise the secondhand department was deserted. Willie's mother's chair was empty though her knitting lay beside the till. He went down the spiral staircase. At the bottom, a door which he had noticed before was standing slightly ajar; he pushed it open without knocking and came upon a tableau which interested him. Iris, Willie and his mother in attitudes which they held as though petrified. The old lady had an unhealthy flush, Iris was pale, Willie looked sullen. The room was a little office and in contrast with the gloom of the flat which he had just left, it was gay with reflected sunlight, the ceiling and walls brilliant with dancing patterns of light from the waters of the harbour outside. He must have blinked foolishly in the doorway. The old lady was first to recover. 'You wished to speak to me, superintendent?' Precisely the right blend of courtesy and rebuke. He had to admit to a grudging admiration, and yet she had made a substantial contribution to the wrecking of two lives and, perhaps, to the premature ending of a third. But was it fair to blame her? No doubt she had told herself that she had to provide the drive which Willie lacked. No doubt she had said the same of his father. Perhaps she was right.

'I want to talk to your son, Mrs Collins.'

Willie seemed to awake from a trance. 'To me? Then we'd better go upstairs.' The old lady made a move but he added, 'No, mother!' He followed Wycliffe out, leaving the two women together.

Willie's room was as gay as the office. Wycliffe sat himself in a chair facing the window while Willie took the swivel chair by his work table. He had been busy, the table was covered by a large sheet of cardboard on which a large-scale map had been drawn and in one corner a legend: *Austerlitz: December 2nd. 1805*. Fragments of card in various shapes and sizes with evocative labels were pinned to the map. Willie had sought refuge from reality in the reconstruction of one of Napoleon's most famous victories.

'So the money came from your aunt.' Frontal attack.

'She told you!'

'She had no option. Now, Mr Collins, last time I was here you told me that you hadn't seen your wife since she left the town. Now you will have to tell a different story so make sure this one is the truth.'

Willie looked older and vaguer, it was impossible to know whether his attention had been gained, whether he understood the seriousness of his position. Wycliffe suspected that he was too withdrawn, too self absorbed.

'When did you give her the money?'

He looked as though he did not understand the question and made no attempt to answer.

'I have a witness who will say that your wife was expecting a visitor at midnight on the night of her death. He will also say that she was expecting to receive certain money from her husband – from you, Mr Collins.'

The words seemed to be lost on him. He passed his hand over his forehead and murmured, 'I want to know who did that to her; if only I could be sure!'

Wycliffe remembered times in his own life when he had seemed to lose contact with the world outside, to become aware of it only when it obtruded in some unwelcome fashion. At such times he might have voiced his thoughts aloud and been ashamed and irritated if someone overheard and tried to answer. But it was not for him to be sympathetic. 'It is my belief that on Tuesday night, just before midnight, you went to the Marina to give your wife the thousand pounds you had obtained from your aunt. You did this by arrangement with your wife, an arrangement made over the telephone or, perhaps, you discussed it when you met her outside the hotel on Tuesday morning. You were seen talking to her,' he added and Willie did not deny it.

Willie stood up and began moving restlessly about the room. Wycliffe was still not sure how far he had penetrated the depths of his introspection. 'Why did you kill her?'

The thick lenses flashed in the light but Willie said nothing.

'You made love to her, then you strangled her – why? Did she ridicule you? Did she tell you that she had fooled you again? That she had no intention of coming back to the life you could offer her?' There was no doubt now that he had riveted Willie's attention. 'Or did she make you intolerably jealous by taunting you with the affairs she had had with other men? Worse still, were you standing on the fire escape, watching, while she tried to persuade Allen to make love to her?'

He paused and though Willie said nothing his eyes never left Wycliffe's.

'You said yourself that there is a point beyond which the worm will turn. For everyone, according to you, there is a threshold of violence. Did Julie push you over that threshold?'

He was gambling on the assumption that in the five days since Julie's death Willie's guilt had become an insupportable burden, that he would find immeasurable relief in confession. For Wycliffe was satisfied that Willie had killed his wife and equally convinced that he had not mutilated her afterwards. The sight of her in the mortuary had overwhelmed him and Wycliffe believed that eventually the blend of guilt, bewilderment, horror and fear would be too much for him. All his life he had taken his troubles to someone, usually to Aunt Jane; the two of them would 'sit down and work something out together'. Had he gone to her and blurted out, 'I've killed Julie'? From Aunt Jane's manner Wycliffe was inclined to think not. Willie was carrying this, his greatest burden, alone – so far.

He was standing by the shelves where his soldiers were deployed, fiddling with them, shifting one here and another there, then putting them back to their original positions. His hand hovered over a troop of cavalry and he lifted one of the red-coated horsemen and held it, seeming to study the modelling intently. Wycliffe let him be and looked out of the window, watching three tugs fussing round a giant tanker like Lilliputians round a Gulliver.

'She said in her letter that I mustn't come to the hotel until she sent for me but I couldn't keep away. I walked past the place six or seven times on the Monday without catching sight of her, but on Tuesday morning I was lucky, I met her just as she was coming out of the gate . . . ' His voice faltered and he stopped speaking. No doubt he was reliving the moment when he had first set eyes on her after months of separation. 'She seemed no different, it was just as though we had run into one another in the street as we sometimes did when she was . . . when we were living together. She said, "Oh, Willie! this will save me phoning", and she told me what she wanted me to do – to bring the money that night.'

'She had told you in her letter how much?'

He resented the interruption and dismissed it with a nod. 'She told me to come by the fire escape which goes up to the bathroom window at the back of the hotel. There's a footpath which runs along by the railway cutting round the backs of the houses . . . ' His voice trailed off into silence. He put down his horseman and picked up another.

'Did you tell anyone of your appointment?'

He looked at Wycliffe for some time before answering, as though debating in his mind what to say, then, 'I told my aunt.' As he spoke, his hand closed on the little horseman and the delicate metal legs snapped. He opened his hand and looked blankly at the fragments then he allowed them to slide off his hand on to the carpet.

'Why did you kill her?'

No answer.

Wycliffe was conscious of the delicacy of his task, to exert enough pressure to make him talk without reducing him to hysterical incoherence. 'You loved her?'

'She was the only . . . ' He broke off and after a moment said, simply, 'Yes.'

'Have you ever had a blood test, Mr Collins?'

'A blood test?' Surprise, but not apprehension.

'To determine your blood group.'

'Yes, I'm AB.'

'A rather rare group.'

'Yes.'

'The man who had intercourse with your wife immediately before her death was of that group.'

The sensitive mouth twitched but he said nothing.

'It is possible to tell from the semen.'

No response.

Wycliffe was beginning to be oppressed by a curious lethargy. The warm room, the dazzling light, Willie's answer drawn from him laboriously, flat and colourless. He lit his pipe. When he spoke again his manner was friendly. 'You are not the stuff of which criminals are made, Mr Collins. Sooner or later you will find it imperative to talk. Already you are torn apart by a conflict between your instinct for self preservation and an almost irresistible longing to discharge some measure of your guilt by confession and by explanation. To explain – to be able to say, "This is *why* I did it; this is how it happened!"

'Believe me, the conflict is spurious. You cannot, whatever you do, preserve yourself, you have already destroyed the person you were.'

Willie was still standing by the shelves but he was watching Wycliffe and listening. 'Confession, atonement, absolution – is that the formula?' Except for a tremor in his voice the question might have been part of a cosy academic discussion.

'No. Because in my view there is no atonement for murder.'

'A priest would do better.'

'But I am a policeman.' He knew that Willie was on the brink of decision, he knew too that silence would be his best advocate, but at that moment the door opened and Aunt Jane came in.

Wycliffe stood up. 'I think, Miss . . . '

But she turned on him, silencing him with a look. 'I wish to make a statement, superintendent.'

'About what, Miss Collins?'

'I killed Julie.' She spoke triumphantly, the slight smile which so often seemed to hover round her lips was more pronounced, and, as always, it was a smile of satisfaction. 'I killed her, there is no need to torture this poor boy any longer.'

Wycliffe was surprised less by the confession than by Willie's reaction. He gazed at his aunt and in his gaze there was nothing of incredulity or relief or bewilderment, only hatred, and hatred so intense that Wycliffe wondered if he might attack her.

'Well? Are you going to arrest me?'

'I shall need more than a simple assertion of guilt before I do that, Miss Collins.'

'All right! I'll tell you about it. Am I allowed to sit down?'

'Of course!' He gave her his own chair and perched himself on one corner of a built-in cabinet. She sat on the edge of the chair, bolt upright, bony hands clasped in her lap. Her grey eyes seemed more protuberant, her wispy hair more wild. 'I must caution you . . . '

She brushed aside his words. 'When Willie showed me her letter I knew that it would be useless to refuse to help or to argue with him but I was determined that he shouldn't be trapped by that creature a second time.'

Wycliffe glanced across at Willie but he had resumed his seat by the table and his head was bent over his reconstruction of the battle.

'When he told me that he was to see her on Tuesday night I decided to follow him.' She pursed her lips.

Wycliffe looked at the hard embittered features, the

mean mouth, and wondered how the love of this woman differed from that of another. Why should it repel instead of attract? Why should it isolate rather than unite? Because it was selfish? Possessive, certainly, but hardly selfish . . .

'You followed your nephew to the hotel?'

She chose to think that he was doubting her and turned to Willie for confirmation. 'You know that I'm speaking the truth, don't you, Willie?'

But Willie continued to stare at the desk as though he had not heard.

'He came into my room next morning just as it was getting light and saw my wet things. It started to rain just before one o'clock when I was coming back and I got nearly wet through. When Willie opened my door I was awake and he was about to speak when he caught sight of my wet coat spread over the dressing table to dry. I could see by the look on his face that he understood.'

'Understood what, Miss Collins?'

She looked at him craftily. 'That I had followed him.'

Wycliffe waited, but no more came. 'Is this true, Mr Collins?'

Silence for a moment, then the single word, 'Yes.'

This confirmation seemed to be what she had waited for and she continued her story. 'As I said, I followed him when I heard him leave the house just before twelve on Tuesday night. There was nobody about and I had to stay well back for fear of being seen but I knew where he was going so it hardly mattered. I was surprised when he walked right past the Marina but he continued round the corner towards the railway and I understood. He took the narrow path that leads behind the houses on the edge of the cutting and at one of the back doors he stopped and let himself in. After a minute or two I followed. Luckily I waited by the door for a while for it was some time before

I saw him on the fire escape; he seemed to be waiting but after a little while I heard a window opening and he disappeared inside. There was only one light on in the place and that was in the room next to the top of the escape.'

'What did you intend to do? What was the point of following your nephew?'

She gave the question thought, frowning as though in an effort to recall her exact state of mind. 'I'm not sure what I intended to do. I think I meant to wait until Willie had gone and then go in and talk to her . . . I don't know for certain because everything turned out differently. At any rate I climbed the escape and when I got level with the lighted window I could see that it had no blind and the curtains were not drawn so I could look right into the room.' She hesitated and for the first time seemed to have difficulty in going on.

'What did you see?'

She sighed. 'They were both there, Willie and the girl. Willie must have given her the money before I got there and they were talking. She was sitting on the bed in her dressing gown and Willie was standing over her. He seemed to be reasoning with her or arguing, then she started to laugh. She stood up and took off her dressing gown so that she was naked, then she . . . she began to . . . ' She broke off and there were spots of colour in her cheeks. 'I never imagined that any woman could be so degraded!' She made a curious little noise, between a sob and a snort. 'We all know that men . . . She undressed him – literally and I had to watch while . . . And she was laughing all the time, that made it worse. She seemed to be taunting him and even while he . . . while he was under the spell of her lust, she continued to laugh at him and provoke him. I could see that he was angry because there were tears in his eyes and from a child he has always cried when he was angry and not when he was hurt. She was a devil and she deserved to die!' The telling of her story had excited her so that she was breathing rapidly and her hands twisted incessantly in her lap.

He looked at Willie, still slumped in his chair without a movement. Her gaze followed Wycliffe's and for a moment her features softened. Wycliffe looked from one to the other and felt sick. 'What happened?'

'Afterwards he got up and dressed himself . . . '

'Leaving Julie on the bed?'

A moment of hesitation, then, 'Yes, leaving her lying there, watching him.'

'Did she lie still?'

Her eyes narrowed. 'She wasn't dead if that's what you mean. She continued talking to him and laughing.'

'And what did he do?'

'He just dressed and left.'

'And she was alive when he left?'

'Certainly she was alive.'

'What did you do?'

'I was afraid for a moment that he would come out on to the fire escape and find me there but he didn't, he must have left by the front door. The window of the bathroom was still open and I climbed in. When I got to her she was still lying on the bed.'

'She must have been surprised to see you.'

'I suppose she was, I didn't give her much chance to think about it. I stood over her and told her what I thought of her.'

'What did she say?'

'She . . . she called me obscene names.'

'Then you strangled her?'

She looked at him curiously. 'I am a strong woman,

superintendent, she had much less strength than I and it was surprisingly easy.'

'There must have been a struggle.'

'Hardly any.' She stopped for a moment, apparently to order her thoughts. 'I don't think I really meant to kill her. I didn't . . . '

'You were going to say?'

'Nothing.'

Wycliffe studied her gravely, his eyes steady and unblinking. 'Having strangled her, you then battered her face to make it unrecognizable.'

'No.' Again the crafty look. 'I did not. I heard the front door open and shut and footsteps on the stairs. I was frightened because I felt sure that whoever it was would come to her room. I don't know why I thought so but I was right.'

'So what did you do?'

Incredibly, in view of what had gone before, she looked embarrassed. 'I hid in the clothes cupboard.' She gave a self conscious little laugh. 'I hadn't more than got inside when a man came into the room. He called out, "Julie", in a loud whisper. Then he made some joking remark and walked over to where she was lying on the bed. I couldn't see what he was doing there but I heard him let out an oath.'

'Then?'

'Then he went. He went so quickly and quietly it took me a moment to realize that he had gone.' She sighed deeply. 'I came out of the cupboard . . . '

'Did you see the man?'

'Only his back and that not very clearly, I was afraid to open the door more than a crack.'

'Did the man search the room or take anything from it?'

'I told you, as soon as he found that she was dead he

couldn't get away fast enough, but there was one thing, I'd forgotten it until now – he took away her photograph.'

'Her photograph?'

'Yes, one in a silver frame, I noticed it when I was looking in the window and when I came to look for it afterwards, it was gone. He must have taken it.'

'All right go on.'

'I knew what I had to do; if I could prevent that vile woman from causing any more wickedness, I would do it. First I searched the room for anything that would identify her or link her with Willie and . . . '

'But the man had already seen her, lying there – dead.'

She smiled unpleasantly. 'It was obvious that he wouldn't talk. Why didn't he rouse the house? In any case it was a risk I had to take.'

'When you searched the room did you find anything?'

She nodded with satisfaction. 'I found a book of poetry Willie had given her. Apart from the shop label there was an inscription on the fly-leaf in Willie's writing.' She looked across at her nephew, 'I have the book still.'

Willie gave no sign that he had heard.

'It was then that I missed the photograph and realized the man must have taken it.'

'You did not recover your money.'

Her look was enough to tell him that the money had no importance for her. 'I had other things to think about. I had to make her unrecognizable and I was afraid that I should make too much noise and wake the house.'

'What did you use? What weapon?'

'There was a heavy brass weight in the middle of the floor. I suppose they used it as a door stop. It was the weight which gave me the idea in the first place.' She glanced across at Willie and lowered her voice to a whisper, 'I *wanted* to destroy her, she had no right . . . '

'To do what?'

She looked at Willie and back to Wycliffe. 'To live.'

'And having done all this, you walked out. Did you use the fire escape?'

She nodded. 'I went the way I had come.'

'What time was this?'

'It was striking one when I passed the church, just when it started to rain. When I got back here I got out of my wet things and before going to bed I looked in Willie's room. His bed had not been slept in and he was not there. I heard him come in about an hour later.' She looked at Wycliffe challengingly. 'I have told you what happened, superintendent, now you can do what you have to do.'

Wycliffe sat staring at her for a long time but his eyes had lost focus. There was silence in the room except for the noises from the docks and the muffled sounds of traffic in the street. He could hardly believe in the reality of his experience, it was like one of those pointless but infinitely depressing dreams from which one knows there will be an awakening. He stirred himself. 'Mr Collins!'

No response.

His temper was wearing thin. 'Mr Collins! Kindly turn round and give me your attention!'

Willie obeyed and faced him with a blank stare.

'I want to know if you have been listening to what your aunt has told me?'

'I have been listening.'

Aunt Jane watched her nephew with a solicitude which was at once pathetic and nauseating. He avoided her eyes. Wycliffe concentrated all the force of his personality on getting Willie to look at him and to answer his question. 'To the best of your knowledge, is your aunt's account of what happened true?'

Willie stared at the superintendent and the silence

lengthened. Aunt Jane made a small movement as though she would have stretched out her hand to touch him but a frown from Wycliffe stopped her.

'What my aunt has told you is true.'

'You say this, realizing the full implication of her story?'

Another interval. 'Yes.'

'Now, I suppose, you will arrest me,' from Aunt Jane.

'I shall ask you to come with me to the police station and to make a statement. After that we shall see.' He reached for the telephone on Willie's desk and dialled a number. Aunt Jane sat bolt upright on the edge of her chair, serene and content. Willie sat with his head in his hands staring at the carpet.

CHAPTER THIRTEEN

Wycliffe was back in his little office; the clock on the mantelpiece showed a quarter past three and outside the sun still shone. On his desk, two statements, neat little wads of typescript, one from William Reginald Collins, the other from his aunt, Jane Alicia Collins. The two statements corroborated each other in every detail for which corroboration was possible and on the strength of them Jane Alicia Collins had been charged with murder. Jim Gill, who had travelled down overnight, sat on the other side of the desk.

'So it's in the bag?'

Wycliffe was morose. 'You've read the statements?'

Gill nodded. 'I have and it seems watertight to me. What's the matter? Are you afraid they won't stand up in court?'

'I feel sure that they will.'

'Well then!'

Wycliffe stood up. 'She didn't do it, Jim.'

'Didn't do it? But she's made a perfectly reasoned and credible statement full of circumstantial details and Fehling found the weight, locked away in a drawer in her bedroom, with blood and hair still adhering to it . . . '

'And covered with her prints – I know all that, Jim. She battered the girl's face in, there's no doubt of that, but she didn't kill her. I've known from the start that the strangling and the mutilation were irreconcilable, the one came of too much loving, the other from passionate hatred and jealousy.'

Gill took out his cheroots and lit one. 'With all due respect, sir, that's just your reading of the case . . . '

Wycliffe was impatient. 'Read her statement again! It would have been better if you could have listened to her as I did. Circumstantial, as you say, until you come to the bit where she is lying, the bit where she claims to have strangled the girl. Apart from anything else, can you imagine a young and healthy girl being overwhelmed and strangled without one hell of a struggle?'

'You think Collins did it while he was making love to her?'

'I'm sure of it. I very much doubt if he meant to but she was provoking him beyond endurance and unwittingly she reached his threshold of violence.'

'Come again?'

'According to Collins, the point at which the worm turns. Of course, Aunt Jane saw it all through the window and when Willie had cleared out she went in and tidied things up in her own inimitable way.'

Gill studied the ash as it grew on his cheroot. 'If you thought like that, why did you have her charged?'

'What else could I do?'

Gill made a sudden movement which scattered the grey ash over his blue pinstripe. 'Give me ten minutes with Master Willie and I'll give you a confession to beat that one! Little runt, hiding behind a woman's bloody apron!'

Wycliffe smiled. 'He's done that all his life and he's too old to change now. But assuming you got him to talk, what good would it do? Julie's death would blight four other lives – Willie's, his mother's, his aunt's and probably Iris Rogers's too.'

Gill shook his head. 'You mustn't try to play God in this game, Mr Wycliffe.'

Wycliffe looked at him with great gravity. 'I'm not

playing God, Jim, you've got the roles mixed, I'm cast as Pontius Pilate.'

That evening at a little after six, Wycliffe and his wife were sitting near the edge of the low cliff which juts out into the sea to form the main bastion of the harbour, a natural breakwater. The tide had turned but the ebb had not yet acquired strength and the flat calm of the evening flood imparted a stillness to everything encouraging a mood of nostalgic sadness.

'What shall we do tomorrow?'

She turned to him in surprise. 'What about the case?'

'It's all over, Gill and Fehling will deal with the paper work.'

She smiled. 'In that case . . . ' She broke off. 'Look! There's a ship coming out.'

Creeping out of the harbour, a small vessel with gleaming white paint on her superstructure but the black hull gashed with ugly red splashes. The name on her bows was clearly visible: *SS Peruvia*.

'She's bound for Barranquilla, a port in Colombia, and her skipper is a Spaniard called Hortelano.'

'How on earth do you know that?'

'It's a long story!' He leaned towards her suddenly and kissed her.

'What was that for?'

'For being more or less normal.'

THE END